Praise for

Longlisted for the Carnegies Medal for Writing 2026

'Poignant, powerful, often hilarious . . . asks questions about respect, consent and how to hold it together when the plan falls apart.' The *Guardian*

'A resonant and thought-provoking read, unsentimental but warm and funny.' The *Observer*

'A wonderful book about such an important and little-discussed issue, told in such a delicious style. The story is both heartbreaking and uplifting and I want every teen to read it.' Kelly McCaughrain, author of *Little Bang*

'But it's Marnie's journey from rebel without to with a cause that's at the beating heart of the text, and it's both plausible and engaging.' *Irish Times*

'*Not Going to Plan* is a truly hilarious, moving and beautiful novel that captures teenagehood, its pressures and its complexities so perfectly' Margaret McDonald, author of *Glasgow Boys*

'It's great to read a story where threads of useful and accurate information are woven through an engaging, thought-provoking story.' Lisa Hallgarten, Head of Policy and Public Affairs, Brook

'Beautiful, warm-hearted, funny, with teen characters who felt so real. Loved! So sensitively, and brilliantly, done.' Simon James Green, author of *Noah Can't Even*

'This story of teenage pregnancy does not condescend or sugarcoat. It's funny, serious, tender, real – and really, really good.' Rachel Delahaye, author of *Electric Life*

'Gorgeous, innovative and bold writing. UKYA at its finest.' Sara Barnard, author of *A Quiet Kind of Thunder*

'Fisher's groundbreaking book handles multiple big subjects with delicacy, care, and respect for her audience.'
The Irish Examiner

'Once again, I'm in awe. Tia's writing for teens is timely, topical and, importantly, accessible. *Not Going to Plan* should be a staple in every secondary school library.' Sue Cunningham, author of *Totally Deceased*

'This book is in itself a valuable source of help and advice, one that, like *Crossing the Line*, has the potential to change lives.'
Just Imagine

'Another perfectly pitched heart-wrencher . . . It's so important that books like this are written, published, and put into the hands of young people.' Jane Branson, Education Director, Eastbourne Literary Festival

'So much heart, inventiveness, narrative power, as well as humour, and such clever ways of representing the experiences, thoughts and feelings of young people.' Barbara Bleiman, Education Consultant, English and Media Centre

'The visual verse format adds urgency and space to breathe, making it a powerful, relatable read for teens facing big questions.' *The School Reading List*

'Absolutely EXCELLENT! I couldn't stop reading . . . The discussions of identity were so important, as were the highlighting of Harry and acknowledging stealthing for what it is, and reinforcing all the issues surrounding consent. It is all so important and timely.' Sarah Holmes, School Librarian

'Authentic, powerful, and utterly compelling'
Glynn Palmer-Bell, Assistant Director of English at Castle View Enterprise Academy

not GOING TO PLAN

Tia Fisher

Hot Key Books

First published in the UK in 2025 by
HOT KEY BOOKS
an imprint of Bonnier Books UK
5th Floor, HYLO, 105 Bunhill Row, London EC1Y 8LZ

Text copyright © Tia Fisher, 2025
Illustrations by Tia Fisher, based on the concepts by Marnie Staedler

All rights reserved.
No part of this publication may be reproduced, stored or transmitted
in any form or by any means, electronic, mechanical, photocopying or
otherwise, without the prior written permission of the publisher.

The right of Tia Fisher to be identified as author and illustrator of this
work has been asserted by them in accordance with the Copyright,
Designs and Patents Act 1988.

This is a work of fiction. Names, places, events and incidents are either
the products of the author's imagination or used fictitiously. Any
resemblance to actual persons, living or dead, is purely coincidental.

A CIP catalogue record for this book is available from the British Library.

ISBN: 978-1-4714-1837-2
Also available as an ebook and in audio

Typeset by Envy Design Ltd
Printed and bound by CPI (UK) Ltd, Croydon CR0 4YY

The authorised representative in the EEA is
Bonnier Books UK (Ireland) Limited.
Registered office address: Block B, The Crescent Building
Northwood, Santry, Dublin 9, D09 C6X8, Ireland
compliance@bonnierbooks.ie

bonnierbooks.co.uk/HotKeyBooks

For Will and Em, with my love.

Chapter One

MARNIE
Everybody hates me.
I press myself back in the seat.

Mum grips the wheel tighter.
No, they don't.

They do.

But she won't listen and we're nearly here.
The ten-foot-high prison-style electronic gates
swing open with barely a
whisper
and we're sucked inside the Death Star that is
*Wynford Independent
Highly Selective
College for Girls.*

Our cheap little car creeps up the drive,
mindful of the sign that says
Careful of Children Crossing.

Children?
Spawn of Satan, more like.

Marnie, don't mess it up, I'm begging you.
Mum's voice is all flat,
like it got run over.

She sounded different when I was ten,
when I got into Wynford.

Back then, she screamed with joy.
You passed the entrance test!

She was dancing in the kitchen,
tilting the letter in her fingers
so the gold crest sparkled
like a party invitation.

Better yet, you got the scholarship!
She high-fived me.
*Boarding school is such a great chance –
a chance to get away from here.*

She meant away from this particular postcode,
from the smell of poverty and no-hope
clinging to the walls of the bus stop
like grease in a chicken shop.

She had a point,
but I hated Wynford College all the same.
After four and a half years of
feeling homesick, of not fitting in,
I know
it doesn't matter
how small the space, how lazy the landlord,
or how black the mould spores
on the winter walls –

home is home.

Just keep your nose clean,
Mum says now, crunching the gears.
Stay out of trouble until the exams are over.
It's less than two more terms.

'Fewer,' I say –
to piss her off,
even though she wasn't wrong –
'Fewer' than two terms. Not 'less'.

Mum's mouth snaps shut so hard
her teeth clack in her skull.

Grammar-flexing.
That's what sixty thousand pounds of
someone else's money
gets you.

The girls at Wynford College
knew I was a charity case
the minute I opened my mouth,
but what really bugged them
was how I didn't
know my place.

It's not your accent, one girl said,
moving my bed to the draughty corner.
It's your attitude we don't like.

I know I shouldn't generalise, but honestly,
Wynford girls are such
bitches.

That first night of Year 7
I lay awake under scratchy blankets
listening to the mouth-breathing
of seven hostile strangers
and learned to cry
as quietly as
a lie.

Mum pulls into the car park to the left of reception.
You're so close now, she says,
narrowly missing the bumper of a Land Rover.
Just get your GCSEs and stay out of trouble.
No more floral foofies, please.

FOOFIES?
Please tell me she didn't say *foofies*?
Mum's a nurse. She shouldn't be coy.

She means my GCSE art coursework.
I've chosen the topic of FREEDOM.
I'm working on a *homage*
to Georgia O'Keeffe,
a
bold
vibrant
affirming
celebration of
female sexual freedom –

which Wynford College, of course,
deems completely inappropriate to submit.

I fold my arms and stare out of the window
as our crappy tin can creaks
between the rows of glossy SUVs.
I think I'm the last to arrive –
there's already a parade of parents
pouring down the entrance steps.

We're late because I hid the car keys –
which only worked
till Mum negotiated a prisoner swap
with my phone.

I shade my eyes against the February sun
while Mum makes a
monumental mess of parking.

Something's up.
The crowd has stopped.
They're pointing at the lawn, that
precious rectangle
of bright green
(Keep Off The)
velvety grass.

As the strangled vowels
of upper-middle-class outrage
spiral into the freezing air,
I remember that thing I did last autumn.

Oops.

It was months ago.
I nicked a ton of bulbs
from the gardener's shed.
Thought I'd planted duds actually.
Who knew nature took so long?

But now spring's sprung my swear words
from their trap. It's interesting
how the ugly f-word
can look so pretty
spelled out in the
colourful language of
crocus.

The very next day I'm being *de-selected*.
They know it was me.

Perhaps I shouldn't have ticked
Horticulture
on the careers options form?

Apparently my flower display
was just the final daisy in the chain.
I had been warned before.
Many times.

'Froggy' Norton,
the Head Warden,
opens his flabby mouth
and flicks his sticky tongue
around the word *excluded*

before coming out with
managed move
instead.

Marnie Staedler, he says with relish,
you are just too much of a
disRuption.
You will have to take your exams elsewhere.

You will need to show
a real commitment to change before
Wynford Independent
Highly Selective College for Girls
can allow you back for sixth form.

Come back *here*?
He has to be kidding.
Turns out my middle digit can talk crocus too –
I must have green fingers.

Mum takes time off work that she can't afford
and drives to Wynford to fight my case,
but the governors have heard about me.

My raised middle finger,
my customised school uniform,
my self-expressions in shaving foam,
the painted political protest pinned to the noticeboard,
the empty vodka bottle in my bin, vapes in my drawer,
compass ear piercings, stick and poke tattoos,
rainbow-coloured plaits down to my waist,
and the fee-paying parents' faces
when they set eyes on
the message I'd
embedded
into the
grass.

The governors say, *No.*

I say, *That's discrimination!*

On what grounds? Mum asks,
shrugging off her best coat
in the hall.

Age? It's a protected characteristic after all.

I don't think 'teenager' counts, Mum says,
and leans her forehead against the front door,
like her face suddenly got
too heavy.

If I wasn't sure before
who my mum was maddest at –
me or the school –
I'm pretty certain now.

Mum says I've really
crocused-up my career prospects.
I'm terrified
she could be telling
the truth.

I can't even figure out
how to say I'm sorry,
but I don't need to worry –
Mum's got it all worked out.

She says I need to face the
consequences of my actions,
learn to think before I act.

Tough love, she calls it, and she
makes me ring up the local comp
and tell them I've been
kicked out
excluded
manage-moved.

The secretary of Downham High
has blocked sinuses.

I ask if they'll let me in,
just for seventeen weeks
so I can take my GCSEs.

She asks me why I lost my place at Wynford.
Nosy cow.

I dig my nails into the
Play-Doh of my arm
and grind my teeth through a
censored version of the truth.

She listens to the whole
humiliating story
before she tells me
it's already been arranged:
I start after their half-term.

Well, thanks a bunch, Mum.

You're welcome, Mum says,
scraping out the peanut-butter jar.
Think of it as paying penance.

At least I don't have to tell Dad.
The last time I tried to ring him
I got number unobtainable.
Mum said that sounded about right.

The email arrives.
I start at Downham High School in a week.
Ofsted reckons the school requires improvement . . .
Maybe they think my grades will help?

But it was having more than half a brain that got me into so
much trouble at Wynford.
They say they want you to think for yourself,
but they don't –
not really.

It's weird being out of school.
I swiped some pens and paints from Wynford
so I could do some coursework,
interpret my new-found *freedom*
through the medium of art.
But I don't feel very creative.

Mostly I wander lonely around my town,
freaking out about my GCSEs.

In the library, the refugee kids
crowd around a study book
like it's an open fire,
warming their heads with knowledge that's
cheaper than fuel,
waiting for their number to come up
on council waiting lists.

I don't talk to them,
because what would I say?
Sorry?

Sorry
that they have risked their lives
for the chance
I've simply

thrown away?

Chapter Two

ZED
Teenage life forms
    bump against me as I spin
    the Fibonacci sequence
    to crack open my locker.

Four & a half years
    of being digested in this ecosystem,
trapped inside the noisy, smelly gut of Downham High,
pushed along the intestinal tract of education,
by the peristalsis of the syllabi.

I'm nearly through.
Only a term & a half to go
    before the colonic squeeze of GCSEs
    pushes me out like a –

Sh*t!
Omar Jones slams his hand against a locker door.
I didn't do my physics!
Ms Rahman's gonna steam me for sure.

No doubt about it, I agree.

There are one thousand & sixty-three students
    at Downham High,
    which is just above the national average –
    unlike our results.

The twenty-three students in 11R
    sit two
    to a desk
    every desk full
    except for one
    empty seat beside   me.

Actually,
>   that suits me just fine.
I do like my own
>   space.

Soon there will be no more Omars.
I'm aiming at a super-selective
>   scientific sixth form,
a sure-fire springboard to Oxford.

I watch 11R bouncing around,
rubbing up against each other's desks,
creating so much *friction* as they
>   jostle against each other, modelling
>   atoms in a liquid state.

My classmates never get tired of
>   talking, boasting, joking, flirting.

A stink of body spray
>   has to fight against
>   the daily assault of hormones.

Some of the sexual bragging
>   might be true, but
>   most undoubtedly isn't.

I don't care.
If anybody was to
>   ask me how I spent my
>   half-term break,
I'd have to say I left the house just once:
>   to purchase the three hundred jelly babies
>   I judged to be sufficient
>   to see me through my
>   programme of revision.

Harry Borman holds court, with
    one leg hitched on Rakel's desk,
flashing a white sports sock
    as he riffs on her virginity,
talking mostly to her chest.

Rakel tells him to piss off,
& his girlfriend Jessica
    calls him back to heel with
    the dog whistle of a
    dirty look.

Omar Jones is laughing in the corner,
    homework all forgotten –
    again.

Hey, Zed!
Luca Moreno swans by my desk,
    slapping it lightly,
    the current of air he creates
    lifting the papers
    ever so slightly.

In his wake,
    they are minutely disarranged.

I don't reply.
I'm not so keen on conversation.
It has all the
 unpredictability of ping-pong.
Between the opening serve &
the ricochet of reply,
words can go

anywhere.

That's why, on the whole,
 I prefer to keep
 my thoughts
 to myself –

especially the ones about Luca.

Chapter Three

3

MARNIE
Mum's on earlies, so
I don't even get a lift to school
on my first day.

I suck hard on my vape as
three buses sail straight past,
the windows packed with
dark blue Downham uniforms,
the odd *help-me* face of a
hijacked commuter
pressed against the glass.

The fourth bus
spits me out by the school fence,
scrunched-up paper coffee cups
plugging its diamond mesh.

I join the walk-running, under-breath-swearing
stragglers with their back-bumping bags
hurrying up the long path
by muddy playing fields
to reception.

On the right,
a crumbling concrete wall
is daubed with half-scrubbed swears,
sprayed signatures and crappy cartoons.
It's studded with dark red streaks
that could be where the talentless taggers
were lined up and shot –
but I'll have to trust
it's rust.

First discovery. All schools stink –
doesn't matter what class you're in.

Downham smells of disinfectant
and dinners and rubber and armpits and feet.
Close my eyes and I could be back in Wynford
but for a brand-new odour . . .
boys.

When I step into the glass-topped entrance atrium,
its welcome screen spattered by spit balls,
I'm battered by the bass note
bouncing off the paint-peeling walls . . .
boys.

I plaster a *what-you-looking-at?* mask on my face,
but no one so much as glances my way, not even the
boys.

Along with free school meals
I got a new (old) uniform, gifted by the PTA.
The skirt's too long
so I've rolled the waistband up,
and there's a big gob of gum
stuck to the blue blazer,
but at least it covers my
see-through-thin
supermarket shirt.

I'm in Ms – *Mizz not Miss* – Rahman's class.
I hunt for Level 3, Room 5.
By the time I find it,
I'm late.

ZED

Lately, Ms Rahman's been giving us
    the same pep talk on revision
    every morning,
on *repeat, repeat, repeat,*
    repeat, repeat, repeat,
    repeat, repeat, repeat . . .

Reading from the wellness script,
she parrots empty words
    about not getting stressed,
    about keeping it in perspective,
    about taking lots of breaks –

but behind the words lies
    her utter panic
    at our likelihood of success.

She's not talking to me, obviously,
    so I don't listen.
Instead I slip my headphones on
& shuffle numbers in my head,
    working on the most unsolvable problem
    known to the world of maths,
    the *Collatz conjecture*.

I'm manipulating digits
when the classroom door bangs open
& a random girl rushes in,
sudden as a gust of wind.

Ms Rahman looks up. *Ah, Marnie.*
She smiles at her.
Sit at the back, please.

MARNIE
My class tutor smiles
from the frame of her hijab.
She waves me to the only empty seat,
right at the back.

It's all about first impressions.
I have to set the tone,
don't let them smell my fear.

Here goes. Hips forward, and

> I style
> it down
> the catwalk
> alley through
> the tables. Each
> upturned face has
> eyes on me like I'm
> some kind of monster
> so I just glare right back.

ZED
The stranger has a nest of snaky plaits
& a stare to set stone.

She strides towards me.
Whispering rustles like leaves in her wake.
I remove my headphones
    in alarm.

This is Marnie Staedler, Zed,
    says Ms Rahman,
    the new girl I said would be joining us.
Please make her feel welcome.

But the girl's arrival is news to me –
although I might just possibly
not have been listening.

MARNIE
Some scholarship girl I am.
I should've been smart enough
to realise there'd be kids here
from my old primary.

Psst!

Even five years on,
I'd know the smile of little Luca Moreno,
sitting third row back –
except he's not so little now.

He winks a familiar dark eye at me
& mouths, *Marnie?*

I turn my head and – *oh my God!*
there's Jessica Bates.

Jessica Bates.
Bad news.

It probably *was* me
who gave her head lice in Year 5,
but the way she carried on
you'd think it was the plague.
She proper nit-shamed me.
Gave me full-on PTSD
in return.

By the time I reach the only vacant spot,
my nose is so high in the air
I nearly miss my seat.

I plonk myself next to a boy
with a white face and glasses.
He looks horrified.

ZED
The new girl
thuds into the seat beside me &
slams her open bag down
on what is actually *my* desk.

The bag tips open &

a tampon makes
a cunning bid for freedom, but I intercept it
before it's seen.

Ms Rahman claps hands for eyes front.
I observe how Jessica Bates & the new girl
side-eye ⟷ side-eye
each other
right through registration.

MARNIE
Jessica Bates and I stare each other out.
My heart is hammering.

I don't know why she
hates me so much – after all,
I gave head lice to half the class
and no one else acted so scratchy.

She nudges the girl beside her,
points at me and whispers.

Nice.

ZED
The new girl in the seat beside me
smells unpleasantly
of strawberries.

MARNIE
The boy in the seat beside me
keeps his head turned away
like I've offended him.

At the final *Yes, miss!*
the hooter goes like a starting gun.
Kids scrape back chairs,
charge for the door.

I haven't a clue where to go,
so I play for time,
pretending to look at my timetable,
hovering while
Ms Rahman speaks to a dark-skinned boy
with a fade and a scowl.

He throws his hands up in protest.
She frowns, her sunny beam
gone behind a cloud.

I'm so new
I don't even know
whose side I'm supposed
to be on.

ZED
On the way out of class,
    whatever-her-name-is
    pauses.

She watches Ms Rahman
    ripping into Omar yet again
    about his admittedly
    suboptimal
    grades.

I find I'm still holding her tampon.

                                MARNIE
                    The skinny boy taps my shoulder.
                          Hello, he says.
                              I'm Zed.

ZED
Hi, **she says,** *I'm Marnie.*
I nudge my closed hand
closer.

                                MARNIE
                    He tries to shake my hand –
                          which is so weird
                              until
                            I detect
                        the bullet shape
                        nestled in his palm.

ZED
I watch her expression change
    as I palm her the period protection.

You dropped it, I say quietly,
to save any potential embarrassment.

MARNIE
You dropped it, **he says, and**
I think I might die.
I need to change the subject, pronto.
Your name's ZED? I ask him.
Zed as in ex-why-zed?

ZED
Or 'Control Zed', perhaps?

MARNIE
He's seriously weird.
Funny name, I say,
accidentally out loud.

ZED
Funny name, **she says,**
somewhat rudely.

MARNIE
Short for Zebedee Donovan, **he says,**
and he lifts an eyebrow
in challenge.

Boy's got *cojones*, I'll give him that.
Long hair drops down his back
in a single plait.

Thanks, I say and smile.
Thanks, Zed.
He nods.

Periods One and Two
I'm hauled into
hundreds of hasty assessments.
The new school's panicking with
so little time to jump me
over the hurdle of
my GCSEs.

If they put me back a year,
I'll mess up more than their rankings,
I swear.

Not every school, it turns out,
makes you do Latin for GCSE,
which is sort of a pity
because
here I'll have to do
full-on physics instead.

Maybe the only
integrated part of Wynford
was its science course.
Chemistry and biology
were like the crutches keeping
physics on its feet.

I tell them straight off I'll flunk it.
I was almost chucked off the course
last year, for freestyling the circuits practical.
Apparently, sticking my scissors in a socket
and blowing all the lights in the block
wasn't the outcome
we were after.

But Downham makes me
sit a test anyway, and
I write $E=MC^2$ in all the gaps
where my knowledge should be.
One of them's got to be right.

I get a guided tour.
It sure is a long way from Wynford.
There's no oak panelling or
small spacious classes: here
students are sardine-squashed
into crummy classrooms, one with
broken chairs piled up in a corner.
The teachers look mildly harassed.

This school smells and looks like
a pair of worn-out trainers
you couldn't sell on
Pre-loved.

In the toilets,
the walls are so thin
I can hear the trickle of
the urinals from next door.

I keep telling myself
I just have to get through
the exams.

Still, there's hope –
the art and design block
at least smells like it should,
of paint and glue and white spirit.

Maybe here I can spread my wings,
fly free, be *me* in a way that
I couldn't be at Wynford?

Then I meet the art teacher,
and all hope dies.

Mr Challoner is a ferrety little man
in a brown apron, who nods nervously
and flicks his hand
at the clumsy sketches on display –
a series of poorly drawn *Davids*
with the naughty bits air-brushed out.
Good, aren't they? he says.

They're seriously not.

I watch him handing HB pencils
out to his class as though
they were precious jewels,
and my heart heads for the basement:
Mr Challoner makes my old art teacher
look positively *avant-garde*.

I catch the eye of a
tan-coated young woman
washing brushes in the sink,
rainbow hair clips holding back her fro.
As Mr Challoner opens a box of rubbers,
I think she winks at me
complicitly.

Is she our art assistant?
Hope so.

Joining the queue for lunch,
bumped by the barrage of elbows and rucksacks,
I slip behind a harmless-looking
Year 10 segment of the snake
and s_h_u_f_f_l_e forward
until
Jessica Bates struts past
with a pack of other girls in
non-regulation eyelashes,
& my name gets twisted into a weapon.

I leave the line before the burger
hits my plate.

Hunched by the bins,
I eat my chips slowly.
What a waste of a
free school meal voucher.

I'm sorry, Mum.
I'm sorry you've got to find
the extra for my food and heat,
the bus fare and revision books.

I'm sorry I messed
up all those dreams
you had for me.

Chapter Four

ZED
I saw the new girl at lunchtime
>   sitting on her own by the rubbish bins,
>   both looking
>   too contaminated
>   to touch.

I wondered if I should sit by her
>   but her face was unreadable
>   so I slipped into my customary spot,
>   reasoning she might also need
>   a little quiet time
>   to recalibrate.

I might not have been listening
when Ms Rahman warned me,
& obviously there were no other free desks,
>   but still it was a shock, having
>   my space invaded like that.

I'm not *totally* inflexible,
>   but I do prefer to be prepared.

To get my balance back
>   I return to the number sequence
>   that's been going up & down
>   in my head all winter.

The Collatz conjecture is a riddle.
If a number is even, divide it by 2.
If a number is odd, multiply it by 3 & add 1.

No one has ever found a starting number
where the sequence doesn't *eventually*
finish in an endless loop of 4 – 2 – 1.

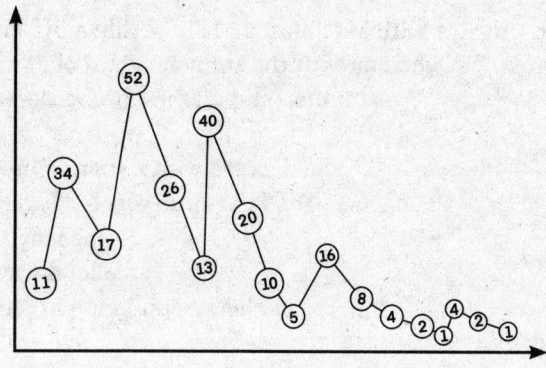

The chance of finding a maverick digit
which produces a different result
  is vanishingly improbable
since supercomputers have failed –

but I find the pursuit both
        fascinating & comforting
                in equal measure.

MARNIE
It's sort of interesting
    how tiring it is
    to keep a sneer
    where a smile could be.

Like getting into a cold sea,
this day gets more uncomfortable
      the deeper I go.
I don't know the in-jokes,
who are the untouchables,
which teachers to avoid.
I don't know *anything*.
When everyone cracks up laughing,
      I stay straight-faced.

In physics with Ms Rahman, I sit beside a big girl
who stares at the shiny patch of old gum
stuck on the fabric of my sleeve.

She digs me with a sharp elbow.
You're wearing my old blazer!
she laughs,
on a loud wave
of cheese-and-onion breath.

We are in the bottom set.
I ask her where Zed is.

*With Dr Allinger and all the other
super-nerds*, she says,
making it sound like a
bad place to be.

ZED
The Doc staggers & leans heavily
on the periodic table.

Zebedee Donovan! he gasps, one hand
hammering his heart, the other one
holding my hand-in.
Only ninety-two per cent!
You dropped eight marks!
However can you live with
such imperfection?

He finds himself so much more amusing
than we do. But I admit
I'm a little perturbed,
until I examine the paper.

It would have been one hundred per cent
    but Dr Allinger misread
    what I'd intended
    to convey.

Happens all the time.

As we file past his desk,
The Doc looks up through
    lenses thick as ship's portholes,
    & calls me back.
Zed, hold up! Some good news!
    he says perkily.
You're through to the Physics Marathon!

The British Schools Physics Marathon.
A series of national endurance tests
    for only the most *elite* of math-letes.
The winners are invited to
    a physics summer school at Oxford University,
    the dreaming spires
    to which I aspire.

My heart beats a little faster.

Dr Allinger says
    my qualifying test got the highest score
    the school has ever seen –
although perhaps that says
    more about the school
    than me.

MARNIE
¡Hola!
says the Spanish tutor,
and I wince.
Wherever Señor Lewis comes from,
it certainly isn't Spain.

Half the group
offer him an *¡Hola!* back,
so he's about midway
in the teacher popularity stakes.

ZED
Señor Lewis shuffles his seating plans
    like a croupier.
I get dealt a good hand today.
Luca Moreno flops down next to me.
¡Hola, cariño! he says with a smile.

Luca's all long bony wrists &
    sharp hipbones, a shock
    of floppy fringe over eyes
    the colour of Marmite.

Luca's parents are from Spain,
    which apparently isn't cheating.

Señor Lewis uses him like a
    portable defibrillator,
resuscitating the Spanish
    as it dies upon our lips.

MARNIE
A boy from my tutor group talks to me
in Spanglish. *Hola, I'm Harry. ¿Cómo estás?*

I say I'm fine. I'd be finer
if I wasn't choking on Lynx Africa,
but he's really fit – at least
in a rugby-player sort of way.
Short shiny hair. Solid thighs. Good teeth.

Let's have a warm-up!
Señor Lewis says,
and we practise the past tenses
I mastered ages ago.

Behind me, I can hear
Zed's tongue slipping on the
icy puddles of foreign phonemes.

ZED
Telling Luca what I did yesterday
   isn't as simple as it sounds.
Spanish is the only subject I struggle with.

People who say
      languages are logical
            are lying.

At the table in front,
   I watch Marnie's mouth moving
   effortlessly around the
   castanet sounds of Castilian.

Señor Lewis's chubby cheeks
    go pink with pleasure.
¡Muy bueno! he exclaims to her,
    way more times than necessary.
If only all my students
    were like you!

He looks in my direction.
I look at the door.

The school day's done.
Across the playground, a bitter wind
    plays hockey with the litter:
the crisp packets & sweet wrappers
    my peers appear
    to shed like skin cells.

I have written to
    the school council,
    the senior leadership team
    & the board of governors
        about the litter situation,
but nothing whatsoever has changed.
My efforts are unappreciated.

Mother said I was
    flogging a dead horse.
Rather a disturbing metaphor,
    I thought.

I dress for the journey home
    in this year's winter gear,
    which has so far been
    most effective at keeping out the chill.

A grey scarf, grey gloves,
    grey parka & a pair of
    cheeky Pikachu earmuffs.
I am as sensitive to cold
    as I am (apparently)
    insensitive to fashion.

As I unlock my scooter
    from the rack,
Harry Borman swings a meaty thigh
    high over the crossbar
    of a flashy racer.

He smirks at me.
Fancy a race, fag?

I laugh at his feeble jibe
    & wave him on.

I have a system.
My left leg scoots me to school,
    my right leg gets me home.

I might not have *meaty* thighs
    but I do like them to match.

MARNIE

Watch out!
I shout a warning
but it's too late.

There's a three-way pile-up
by the sign that says 'No Cycling'.

A boy on a scooter trying to avoid a boy on a bicycle giving a lift to a girl glued to her phone.

The girl turns out to be Jessica Bates.
She shrugs off my helpful hand
with a scowl.
No bones are broken
but her phone screen's cracked –
and being Jessica Bates,
the minimum she wants
is blood.

She says it was all Zed's fault –
but unluckily for her,
I'm a witness.

Zed salvages his scooter,
(old-school, not electric)
and straps on an army helmet
over hideous yellow earmuffs.

He's *unbelievably* uncool.

As I give my statement to the teacher,
Jessica's glare digs between
my shoulder blades,
sharp as her shellacs.

Here we go again.

ZED
After the dressing down,
I turn to thank Marnie
    for her intervention –
    but the new girl's

        gone.

Chapter
Five

ZED
When I get home,
    voices are leaking
    through the study door.

My mother has just been promoted to
    systems engineer for a big bank;
    she's always in online meetings,
discussing the direction of data.

She is currently talking
    across the other tinny voices.
I detect a note of annoyance.

Not everyone's as clever as she is –
I know how she feels.
It's a source of constant
    irritation for us both.

I make myself
a mug of hot milk &
    scrape Marmite across toast.

MARNIE
When I get home, I find Mum's left a
caterpillar chocolate cake on the table,
like it's my birthday
and I'm five.

I slide my thumb under the cardboard
and cut a massive wedge.
No point in dainty slices,
seeing as the use-by date
is today.

The two-days-before-payday
free food-bank fare?
Fine.
Cake is cake.

How did it go, love?
Mum calls from the living room.
Her feet hang over the end of
our sagging two-seater sofa.
An empty tea mug's
balanced on the back.
She's still in her navy nurse's tunic.

Mum's a bank nurse –
which doesn't mean she
nurses in a bank, unfortunately,
because that might pay more.
She fills the gaps in hospital rotas.

But there's often a gap between
what she earns
and what we need,
hence the food bank.

It went, I say,
shovelling in a forkful,
meaning,
I don't want to talk about it.

Well, it was bound to be difficult, she says,
meaning,
What else did you expect?

ZED
My milk has hardly cooled to
    its optimal temperature
    before Mother appears
looking somewhat distracted,
    tablet in hand.
Her normally spirit-level fringe
    is at least fifteen degrees
    off horizontal.

Zed! she says,
as though surprised
    to find me there.

Mother!
I respond, with
    a Vulcan salute.

She flaps my greeting away.
Rude.

Haven't you got homework?
    she asks, like she asks every night.

Of course I've got homework,
    I say, like I say every night.

I tell her I got through to the Marathon.

She nods her confirmation that
qualifying for the top student physics
    competition in the country
    is exactly what she expected of me.

We eat the vegan lasagne that
    we eat every second Thursday
    in comfortable silence.

Upstairs, I slip on
    state-of-the-art, noise-cancelling
    fake-suede headphones.

I want the white noise
    of all the frequencies
    played at exactly the same intensity,
    cancelling out the cars, the fox screams,
    the sirens & other assorted sounds,
so I can concentrate on

    pure

        unadulterated

            physics.

MARNIE

Mum says
Mum says
Mum says
Mum says
Mum says
Mum says
Mum says
Mum says

Exam grades are like rungs on a ladder, the more rungs you have, the higher you'll climb.

> She
> always says,
> *I'll boost you from
> behind, of course, but
> you need to pull **yourself** up.*

On the fridge, she's stuck my
grades from the autumn exams.

Now it feels like they're mocking me.

I start on the hill of homework.
It's English, Spanish and physics tonight.
I level the languages inside half an hour,
but physics is a mountain I just can't climb.

I spend forty minutes displacement-doodling,
making a line of Georgia O'Keeffe-y
flowery vulvas
linking left to right across my tattooed desk
because I have absolutely no clue
what the questions
even *mean*.

Chapter Six

MARNIE
I arrive at school early today.
The vape clouds at the entrance
smells as enticing as a sweet shop.

I take a deep breath and
hang with that crowd for a while.
They all want to know my story.

Mum said I should make a good start,
don't let on I was kicked out,
but I think she's bonkers.

Make out like
I'd left my highly selective
single-sex boarding school
just for the kicks?
Yeah, right.

I let the word *exclusion* leak out.

What did you do?

Were you stealing stuff?

Did you hit a teacher? *Was it drugs?*

I'm not going to rob myself
of this currency. The way I see it,
excluded makes me *exclusive*.
Not to be messed with.

Excluded. I'd wear it
on a button badge if I could,
like a tiny shield.

>   **There's a skinny figure,**
>   scooting past the crowded pavement in
>   a <u>dead straight line</u>,
>   his tiny wheels hemming the road
>   a precise ▼ from the kerb.
>   one metre

> I'd know those yellow flaps anywhere.
> Zed really should ditch those Pikachus.

ZED

I wear these earmuffs to school
   because ears lack insulating fat –
hence the cooling system of elephants.
Without them, scooting would be chilly.

Marnie steps out from the crowd of vapers
   gathered by the gates.

Hi, Zed! she says.
Marnie, I reply.

My breath only condenses a
   discreet cloud around the word,
whereas Marnie appears to be actually *on fire*,
   belching out a thick
   volcanic plume.

A chemical stink surrounds her.
Today's choice appears to be
   cinnamon.

MARNIE
Before I can follow Zed,
there's a skid of wheels
and the boy from yesterday's bike crash
is blocking my path,
poking his handsome face
much too close
to mine.

Hello, Marnie! the boy racer says,
flashing perfectly straight teeth.
It's the Spanish-class Adonis.

It's Harry! he says,
flipping his hair off his forehead.
From your class – from yesterday. Remember?

I remember.
I'm about to tell him he's supposed to
wear his aftershave (not bathe in it),
when I realise
my back is cramping
and there's a horrid, familiar,
sticky feeling in my crotch.

Um, yeah, hi, bye! I say.
I need to find a loo – and fast.

I walk away carefully, with the
just-got-my-period
thighs-wide
penguin waddle.

ZED
I walk my scooter up the entrance path
    alongside the sprayed & scribbled
    length of brickwork we call
    the *Wall of Words*.

Downham students pause here
    to pass on their malodorous messages
like dogs stopping at a lamppost.

Banksy they aren't. It's not new:
the walls of Pompeii were graffitied
    with words too rude to repeat
    in school textbooks.

Downham's fifty-metre-long
    unofficial noticeboard
    is a little less eloquent
    but otherwise much the same.

Insults, anatomically inaccurate cartoons,
& declarations of eternal love
    that will not last the term.

Before I've reached the bike sheds
Marnie overtakes me,
hurrying towards reception.

MARNIE
I use the loos in the atrium.
By the time I come out of the cubicle,
the familiar drag has
begun in the base of my belly,
and Jessica Bates is by the basins.

As I wash my hands, she's preening herself,
smirking at her reflection next to mine.

Deep breath, Marnie.
This is so stupid.
After five years can't we
bury the hatchet somewhere other
than in each other's back?

Jessica accidentally
knocks her hairbrush to the floor.
It's manky, clogged with long blonde hairs,
but I pick it up and hold it out
like an olive branch between us.

She curls her glossy lip.
Probably infested now, thanks a bunch.

She uses her long talons
like tweezers
to avoid touching my hand
and
drops the brush in the bin.
Clang.

The door swishes shut behind her.

I think it would actually be worth
getting nits one more time
just so I could pass them on to
Jessica
bloody
Bates.

           I stay in the toilets a while
               so I don't have to
                  walk behind

               her bitchy behind

                  all the way
                    to class.

ZED
The hooter goes for registration
   & still there's no sign of Marnie
even though she passed me coming in.

That's other people for you.
They're extremely unpredictable.
Especially, I suspect, Marnie Staedler.

                  MARNIE
            Marnie, sit down, please!
               Ms Rahman's smile
       isn't quite as wide as yesterday's.

      As I take my place beside him,
         Zed shifts his chair back
          and wrinkles his nose.
          What is his problem?

                  I
               lean
            across
         the
     gap.
            You all right?
            I whisper.

ZED
You all right?
   she hisses,
      on a breath
         of sickly
            synthetic
               cinnamon,
just as Ms Rahman calls my name.

MARNIE
He says, *Yes, miss!*
to Ms Rahman
but doesn't answer me.
He's so weird.

I whisper,
Hey, what did I do?

Ms Rahman
interrupts his silence
to shoot us a death-glare.
Marnie! Zed! Stop whispering!
she snaps.

ZED
That was most unfair.
I didn't say a word.
Since I obviously need to be more explicit,
I write Marnie a note.

While I understand it is entirely your choice
whether or not to 'vape', I personally find both the
smell and the entire concept repugnant.
If you insist on exercising your personal freedom,
I have the right to exercise mine
and decline to engage in conversation.

MARNIE
It takes me a while
to decipher Zed's half-page of hieroglyphics.

When I look up,
his eyes are on Ms Rahman,
but a muscle twitches
at the corner of his jaw.

That was his problem?
That's all?
Vaping?

OMG, this boy is so uptight.

ZED
Marnie sighs heavily & tuts
as though I'm being uptight.
I'm not.
I just don't like being polluted.

MARNIE
We have Spanish in period three.
Harry pats the seat beside him.
Helloooo! He makes a show
of dusting off the desk.

Is he flirting with me?

We're supposed to be
creating a presentation on
How to Study (in Spanish)
but all the chat on our table is
How to Have Fun (in English), because
Harry's having a birthday party,
the last fun before the exams,
kind of a big deal.

Harry offers me an invite
in exchange for scripting our speech.
He inks his address on my hand.
¡Numero ocho!
¡Mi casa es tu casa! he adds,
looking disturbingly pleased with himself.

ZED
Luca's grinning at me.
Si. ¡Una fiesta, mi amor!
Harry's place, next Friday.
He scribbles Harry's address on a dayglo Post-it.
Come! It'll be fun.

Did Luca really just invite me to a party?
Did Luca really just invite *me* to a *party*?
I've never been asked to a party before.
Parties are not exactly my thing.

You look like I invited you to an orgy!
Luca whispers.
At the word *orgy*, I feel
    my face burst into flames.

Go on, Zed!
Luca lays his hand on
    the bare part of my arm.
Last chance to show us your moves!

His hand stays there.

Luca's always been queer.
From eleven years old he *owned* it,
    swanning round the playground unashamed.
Maybe coming out's
    like ripping off a plaster –
best to do it quickly,
    all at once.

I turn the address over & over,
    searching for an appropriate response.

His fingertips feel too intimate.
Mine leave damp marks on the paper.

MARNIE
Señor Lewis claps his hands
like a tubby flamenco dancer.
Enough of the chat!
he says sharply. *Marnie! Zed!*
You two sit together now.

ZED
Damn.

MARNIE
Damn.

MARNIE
Harry scowls as I move my stuff.
Well, Zed'll *have* to
talk to me now –
in Spanish at least.

ZED
I will have to speak to Marnie,
but not face to face.

If you think I'm going to inhale
  any more of your vape-breath
  than strictly necessary,
you can think again, I tell her.
If anyone who vapes
  does much thinking,
  which I doubt.

I turn my face
to face a different way.

MARNIE
I don't see why
my vaping is your business,
I hiss at his back.

ZED
I rotate my neck the necessary ninety degrees
  to deliver the putdown.
You really don't know? Ha!
Quod erat demonstrandum!

MARNIE
A comeback in *Latin*?
What a geek.

*I don't really think
that proves your point
at all*, I say.

And
for the rest of the lesson
neither of us says a word
in any language.

Chapter
Seven

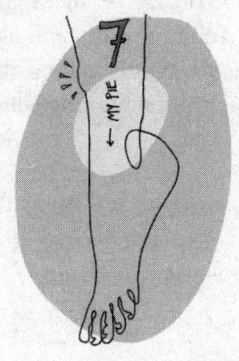

MARNIE
The afternoon timetable
is a killer block of doomy green.

P.E.	P.E.	P.E.	P.E.

At Wynford,
me and the games staff had a deal.
I did their donkey work –
puffing endless circuits of the track
fetching balls and laying out markers,
counting armbands and cleaning mud off bibs,
taking nose-bleeders to sick bay,
moving their goalposts
miles and miles
(quite literally),
and in return
they never
made me
join in
team stuff.

I didn't have to
pick sides –
and
more importantly,
sides
didn't have to
pick me.

To my horror, here at Downham
I'm expected to play *actual hockey*,
even though I have my
actual period.
I'm kitted out
from the lost-property cupboard
and there are no shin-pads.

A bouncy girl with streamlined thighs
picks me for her team.
She's called Rakel.
She has a welcoming smile and no idea
of the massive mistake she's making.

The whistle blows sharp as a slap
and I jog slowly up and down the wing,
keeping as far away
as possible from that
hard-looking ball.

Cold stings my bare legs.
My plaits are whipping my face.
My belly cramps.
This is so not fun.

The centre forward
slips
and
SCREAMS
and stays down in the mud.

I offer my stretchering expertise,
but
Rakel shouts and points,
and before I can run away,

I find myself bullying off against Jessica bloody Bates face to face face to face

ONE

tap!

TWO

tap!

THREE

Bash!!!

Jessica hares off down the field,
leaving me to breathe
through the pain of a blue-bruised shin,
a violently wide
scrape
of broken skin.

With the last of my dignity
I limp off the field,
flapping a hand in answer to Rakel.

I only came here to get my exams,
not lessons in so-called
sportsmanship
from the likes of Jessica Bates.

I always said team sports suck
and this proves my point.
Quod erat demonstrandum,
as I suppose Zed
would say.

The changing room's choking on a fug
of sweat and spray deodorant.
Rakel comes over and asks if I'm okay.

She pokes at the lump sticking up
like an Adam's apple
from my shin. *Does it hurt?*

I wince. *It does now.*

She grins. *Sorry!*

Rakel squints at my ankle,
at the two-word tattoo
I poked so painfully
during prep at Wynford.

Pie is Spanish for *foot*, I explain.
Her forehead knits together in a tiny frown.
Not everybody thinks it's funny.

She changes the subject.
*You and Jessica . . . I hear
you have history?*

I shrug.
She's got some beef from primary, that's all.

We finish dressing side by side.
I watch as Rakel smooths her eyebrows,
combs her straight black hair
and shines her lips.
She's South Asian, super pretty.

Want some?
She throws me the stick.
Sparkles aren't my thing,
but I smear it on thick as
honey on toast.

Rakel smiles. *Suits you.*
She slips a silver crucifix
around her neck.

Although the tiled room echoes
with shouting and laughing
and the tinny whirr of dryers,
Rakel still lowers her voice when she says,

*Hey, I heard Harry Borman
inviting you to his party.*

So? I button up my shirt.

*So you'd better hope
Jessica didn't overhear.*

*Those two have been off and on
since the start of Year 10.*
Rakel looks around her.
*My advice?
Watch your back.
She's vicious.*

I sling my bag onto my shoulder. *I'll cope.*

Rakel walks me to the bus stop and we shout,
See you tomorrow! at each other
from tinselled lips.

It's a squash on the bus.
A football rolls up and down the aisle.
The windows are steamed with swearing.

I send a swift reply to Mum's enquiring text.

> i survived day two! 😊

It could have gone worse:
even if Jessica and Zed are hostile,
Rakel and Harry seem to like me.

I rub a dripping circle on the glass.
Harry's address on my hand
is still just legible.

Jessica Bates might *think*
Harry Borman belongs to her –
but he sure doesn't act like it.

I stuff in my earbuds.

ZED

Even insulated by my headphones,
    it's hard to concentrate on
    homework tonight.

All the white noise in my head
    can't cancel out
    the sound of Luca's invitation
playing on my mind.

I cannot interpret him.
I do not understand myself.
There is far too much uncertainty
    for my liking.

I go downstairs
    to make myself
    a soothing cup of cocoa.

No light shines under the study door.
Mother is out tonight
    at some networking thing for
    successful women,
the kind of women
    who don't need men.

If I'm asked about my father
    I explain I've never met him
    & that usually shuts them up.

I don't feel the need to volunteer
    the whole truth,
which is that my mother has
    never met my father either.

Unlike most people, I'm not just some random
    combination of genes.
My mother went shopping online
    & found a donor
    who looked a lot like her,
with a bonus PhD in atomic physics.

No promises were broken
    in the making of me:
my mother got exactly
    what she asked for.

It might not be conventional,
    but there's a logic
    to my conception:
I was *all* that was necessary.

My mother didn't want to share
    her child
        or her life
            or her body
                with anyone else.

Makes perfect sense to me.

MARNIE
Mum's going on a date tonight.
She parades a dress
for my approval.
It's green – not her colour –
and the charity-shop label says
ten pounds fifty,
which in my opinion
is ten pounds too much.

But I smile and say how nice she looks,
because being nice costs nothing,
and, let's face it,
I owe her.

Mum's bad taste extends to men.
Maybe it's because she's a nurse,
she can't help trying to
heal the ones who can't be fixed.
Broken men look to her for glue,
but no one sticks around for long.

My dad, for example, left when I was small
and Mum was still only
size twelve.

Over the years, his visitations got less and less:
from long weekends to short afternoons,
from video chats to voice calls
to the occasional text,
until eventually
they stopped.

These days, there's not even
a birthday card.
All I have of him is the
cool leather jacket he left behind,
and even that
I had to rescue from the bin.

Mum's given up
trying to get any money out of him.
Like trying to get blood from the stoned, she says,
although it's not funny.

Even Child Maintenance can't find my dad,
and they've been looking for years.

Before she leaves, Mum
makes sure I see her tucking a

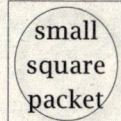

inside her purse.

She winks at me
and I want to die of TMI.
Better safe than sorry, eh?
Don't want any accidents.

Mum says condoms should be used
on every *conceivable* occasion.

She's not sorry she decided to keep
her first and only
accident,
but she doesn't want another.

Can't say I blame her.

Chapter Eight

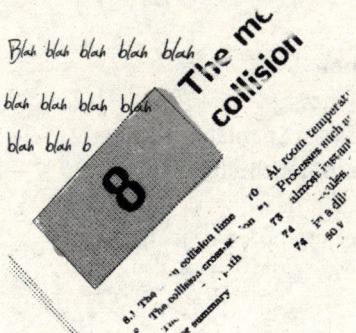

ZED
All that week, I find myself wondering
    about Marnie: perhaps there was no need
    to be quite so abrupt.
There is a possibility I overreacted.
She *did* defend me against Jessica.

MARNIE
All that week,
I wonder why Zed's got such a
problem with me. I sort of liked him
before he threw that hissy-fit.

ZED
Although I do not,
    strictly speaking,
        need a pass in Spanish,
I would still like to get the full set.
Perhaps Marnie can help.
Perhaps I should apologise.

MARNIE
It's a shame because
I could really use
some help with physics.
I need some kind of interpreter,
someone to translate these symbols
into a language I can
understand.

ZED
On Friday I send her an email with
MEA CULPA as the subject.

> **MARNIE**
> **On Friday my school inbox**
> pings with an email which –
> since the subject line's in Latin –
> could only be from Zeebedee Donovan.
>
> Well, at least
> he admits he was in the wrong.
>
> I pull my beat-up laptop towards me
> and accept his apology with grace.
>
> I have a proposal to make.

ZED
In return for bringing her up to speed in physics,
Marnie promises to give me help with Spanish
& also offers bonus
    (entirely gratuitous)
        tips on style.

```
For a start, she writes, no offence, but
   those yellow earmuffs
   have to go.
```

Well, no offence taken, Marnie Staedler,
though I'm not sure I need
    lessons in cool from a girl
    who blew in on the winter wind
    scattering tampons in her wake
    & smelling like a chemical fruit basket –
but I admit
    I do rather like
    how she doesn't like
    Jessica Bates.

As it happens, this is timely.
The application to my new sixth form
    requires a personal statement, but
    to be honest, I don't have much to say.
The box labelled *Outside Skills & Interests*
    remains a vacuum
since I haven't joined anything
    after the crushing disappointment
    that was
    Year 7 Chess Club.

Tutoring will do nicely.

I type back a counterproposal.

```
Provided you desist
from your disgusting habit,
I would be happy to accept.
```

MARNIE
He cracks me up.
You're on,
I reply, typing one-handed,
fingers crossed behind my back.
What he doesn't see
can't hurt him.

ZED
On the colour-coded schedule on my board,
    it's hard to see where
    blocks of being helpful to the new girl
    can be squeezed in.
I draw a line through some periods
    reserved for relaxation.

I need to scope this task.
I send another email.
How much don't you know about physics?

How can I possibly know
    how much I don't know?
    she parries, with a surprising grasp of logic.
That's an oxymoron,
you moron.

Burn. This could be more entertaining
    than I'd thought.

ZED	**MARNIE**
At your place?	**At your place?**
We agree to study at school.	We agree to study at school.
	It's not that Mum would mind me bringing Zed home – she'd probably be thrilled – and it's not that I'm ashamed.
	But there honestly isn't room in my room for two.

ZED
Thank goodness.
I'm not sure what my mother
would make of Marnie.

Chapter Nine

MARNIE
Monday starts with triple art.
Today the art technician's fingernails
are painted all the
colours of the rainbow.
Oh, wow!
she says, chewing gum
and pointing at my
genitalia.

I splodge a final dab of paint
on a violet-shaped vulva
and step back to squint.

A response to Georgia O'Keeffe, right?
She tilts her head.
*So, which GCSE
theme did you choose?*

Er, Freedom.
I would've thought it was obvious.

She laughs an ice-mint breath and
nods at my painting.
And this is freedom . . . how?

It's freedom of . . .
I hesitate.
Well, it's freedom to . . .

Well, to be honest,
I haven't really thought it through.
But I love to shock art teachers
and anyway –
fannies are easier than faces.

The art tech drags a stool to sit beside me.
*I don't think we've been introduced.
I'm Naomi, the art technician.*

She flips through the heavy pages
of my portfolio and whistles.
*You're certainly very bold.
And also – did you know
you're very good?*

I'm walking on air
all the way to my
Spanish–physics swap
with Zed.

ZED
Marnie is later than
the margin of tolerance I'd allowed.

I wait for her in a quiet corner of the library,
reviewing the physics questionnaire
I spent one hour & thirty-three minutes preparing
in order to establish her <u>baseline</u>, get
a defined starting point for comparison purposes.
I have made an effort to be user-friendly.

When she arrives, she's unrepentant
even though
I make a show
of checking my watch.
But her grin goes when she sees the
smiley-face options for each of the
Physics GSCE Learning Objectives.

So, how secure, I prompt her,
    do you feel in your grasp of the motor effect?

Are you insane? she hisses.
We don't have time for this!
She scribbles a massive frowny-face
    which obliterates most of the page.
Just assume I don't know any
    of this stupid stuff.

Shhh, please!
    says the sixth-former on duty.

I put the questionnaire away.
Marnie could have been
    a little more appreciative.
That was valuable Physics Marathon
    revision time.

I sigh.
We'll start at the top of the list.

MARNIE
After ten minutes
I think I'm getting the motor effect.

Zed might be a bit weird,
but he's patient. Calm.
Good at explaining.

I understand now, I tell him,
looking at the shiny rope of hair
reaching down his back.

I grab a pencil.

ZED
After ten minutes
I draw the conclusion that
Marnie might be more random
   than Brownian motion,
but she's not stupid,
not at all, she's just a little –

*MARNIE! Would you mind **not** sketching me, please?*

                          – haphazard.

                                MARNIE
                                 Aw.
          Doodling helps me concentrate,
      takes my mind off the absence of
                              nicotine.

ZED
We switch to Spanish.
Marnie can't stop laughing
   at my accent.

She writes *!Hablo español como una tetera!*
& records herself saying it,
   then
       records me saying it,
           then
               cracks up.

Can't you tell the difference? she says,
   jabbing her earbud uncomfortably
   against my lobe.

Yes, I can hear the difference –
> but it doesn't help.
Just because I can *hear* Beethoven,
> doesn't mean I can play
> the Moonlight Sonata.

I don't get how you don't get it!
> *she says. You might have a brain*
> *the size of a planet,*
> *but you **really** suck at this.*

I'm not sure your teaching style
> *is entirely attuned to my learning needs,*
> I remark, quite mildly.

Marnie snaps her gum
> in my face.
Oh, don't get all huffy again!

MARNIE
It's nearly time for period four.
The stream of students passing by
> picks up its pace.

Anyway . . .
I give up and slide the Spanish textbook into
> my falling-apart rucksack.
> *What's more important is –*
> *¿Vas a la fiesta de Harry?*

¿ . . . . ?
Zed asks with his eyebrow.

ZED
Are. You. Going. To. Harry's. Party?
Marnie repeats very slowly in English,
as though I'm an idiot.

MARNIE
We didn't have parties at Wynford.
We had *socials* in the main hall,
awkward distanced dancing
with boys bussed in from the independent.

A bunch of stuck-up snobs
wearing waistcoats – *waistcoats!* –
dancing like they had rulers
stuffed up their bums.
But better than nothing, I guess.

The socials always ended
before things could get interesting –
though that wasn't
for lack of trying
on my part.

Virginity's an itch
you can't scratch
by yourself –
but the furthest I ever got
was a busted bra strap.

It's different at Downham.
The Year 11 Jessica types
lean across the desks
with shirts brazenly unbuttoned.

They sashay down the corridors
rolling their hips like dragnets
to catch the boys –
boys who definitely
don't wear waistcoats.

By the lockers this morning
I asked Rakel to come,
but she shook her head
and pressed her lips into a
flat line of refusal.
My dad wouldn't let me.
Boys and booze before the exams?
Before anything, in fact.
It's a no, sorry.

She didn't sound particularly sorry, but
slammed the locker shut
on any argument.

I'm not missing my first party.
I'll go on my own if I have to.

ZED
Am I going to Harry's party?
Me? The very idea is ridiculous.
She should know full well
 I'm not going to Harry's party.
Of course I'm not going to Harry's party.

Perhaps, my mouth says.

MARNIE
There's only one way to decide.
I pull out a 10p piece.
Heads you do, tails you don't.

I toss the coin up into the air and watch as it comes down........

....

heads.

That's settled then.
I zip the coin back in my purse.
You're going.

Don't be ridiculous!
Zed snaps.

ZED

I point out to Marnie the fallacy
    of relying on chance
    to make an informed decision.

& yet . . . the idea of going
    is growing
    on me.

I say I will consider it.
We leave for lessons.

Dr Allinger seems to think
    physics is the only
    subject on the curriculum.

On Friday evening he sends me a link to the
    Brainiac Boot Camp,
an online prep for the Marathon
which will effectively absorb
    eighty per cent of available revision time.

I mention my concerns to Mother.
She is frowning at something on her screen.
Apply logic, Zed. You're on course for 76 GCSE points.
The Marathon is less than three weeks away.
If you do well, you'll attend
    a summer school with the top 0.01 per cent
    of physics students in the UK.
It will do wonders for your sixth-form application.

My mother has a way of clarifying things.

I'm logging on, limbering up for the boot camp,
    when Marnie messages me.

MARNIE
Zed just needs a boot up the backside.

> come to harry's party!

It will do him good.
Anyone can see that boy
needs to get a life.

> Why?

> i need you there

> Why?

> um, to have fun? dance?

> I don't dance.

Of *course* he doesn't dance.

> i'll teach you

> You suck at teaching.

> please?

> ...

> PLEASE!

> ...

> PLEASE! PLEASE! PLEASE!

I want to HAVE FUN!

I want to MAKE FRIENDS!

I want to GET F—

> Go away please.
> I am actually studying.

But after Marnie's interruption
I don't, actually, study.

When attempting to reach a logical decision,
    a weighted spreadsheet can be very helpful.

However, I find myself
    unable to assign values
    to the criteria in the *Arguments For*.

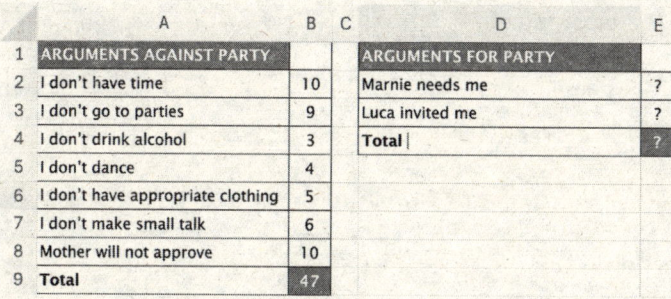

	A	B	C	D	E
1	ARGUMENTS AGAINST PARTY			ARGUMENTS FOR PARTY	
2	I don't have time	10		Marnie needs me	?
3	I don't go to parties	9		Luca invited me	?
4	I don't drink alcohol	3		**Total**	?
5	I don't dance	4			
6	I don't have appropriate clothing	5			
7	I don't make small talk	6			
8	Mother will not approve	10			
9	**Total**	47			

While it is most illogical, irrational,
    to even consider going,
the idea is inexplicably appealing.

My thumb flicks nervously,
    switching my phone screen
        between life & stasis.

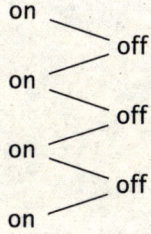

on
      off
on
      off
on
      off
on

My physics textbook lies open on my desk.
A call-out catches my eye.

> Inertia is the tendency of an object to continue in its state of rest or in uniform motion unless acted upon by an external force.

Marnie & Luca are certainly
   a most forceful
   combination.

Chapter Ten

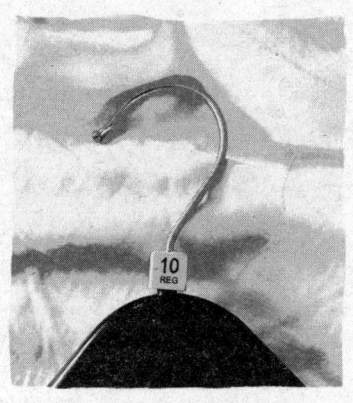

MARNIE

On Saturday I check out my floordrobe.
>I have, like, literally
>no clothes.

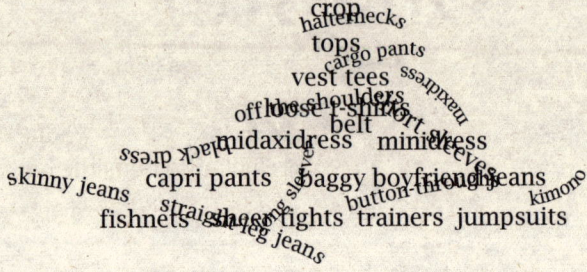

>What am I going to wear?
>Everything makes me look
>fat
>or
>stupid
>or
>fat *and* stupid.

>Mum walks in and eyeballs
>the clothes mountain.
>A twisted jeans leg
>lies limply like a broken limb
>under an avalanche.

>*Yeah, don't start!*
>*I say, before she can.*
>*There's a party next week*
>*and I've got nothing to wear.*
>*Can I go shopping, Mum, please?*

> *It's a shame my clothes don't fit you –*
> Mum taps a nail against her teeth –
> *or you could borrow something.*

> I look at her filling my doorway
> and remember the green dress.
> She has to be joking.

> She was.
> She reluctantly raids the bills jar.
> *I know it's not much*, she says,
> *but try second-hand.*

> Fifteen quid disappears into
> the hungry mouth of
> my flat purse.
> No second helpings allowed.

ZED

When not in my school uniform,
I prefer a *non-school uniform* of
    grey jeans & hoodie.
Up till now, comfort & anonymity
    were all that was required,
but tonight my eyes keep sneaking
    to my wardrobe.

If I went
    (which I won't),
what would I wear?

I look along my stacks of
    Neatly   ironed   hooded
    folded   smooth   sweatshirts
in differing shades of grey.

I have to shake myself back into focus.
I have a test next week &
    less than perfection
    is failure.

MARNIE
Inside the charity shop
it smells of biscuits
left too long in the tin.

I riffle along the rows of mismatched clothes
looking for bargains to fit my budget.
Savvy haggling snags a
a skinny black polo neck
and a lime-green
big-buckled
miniskirt.

At least
Mum and I share a shoe size.
In her black, shiny, over-the-knee, thick-soled
hooker boots and Dad's massive biker jacket,
with my hair unleashed to kiss my waist,
I'll channel super-sassy,
don't-mess-with-me
kick ass.

On Monday I stop at the gates,
sucked into the sweet-smelling cloud.
Considering why
vapes were invented,
it's not actually
that easy
to stop.

ZED
We're in double maths first thing,
    revving our
    mental
    engines.

At least, I am.
Luca's looking
    over the crook of my arm,
copying my calculations.

You are coming to the party, aren't you?
    he asks.

I nod, in the offhand way of someone
    who hasn't been awake all night
    worrying about it.

I'm very much afraid
    there will be dancing.

MARNIE
On Thursday
Harry Borman drops his lunch tray next to mine.
    Looking forward to the party?
        he asks.

Did I say I was even coming?

I make my lips curve at the corner
    just so –
    just like I practised.

    Harry laughs –
    just like I hoped.

I look at him from under my lashes,
tipping my head to duck
Jessica's glare.

My physics homework comes back.
Much better! Ms Rahman has scrawled
at the bottom. *Keep it up!*

I go to thank Zed at lunchtime,
ask him when we can study again,
but he's stony-faced.

Deal's off! he says.
I saw you vaping at the gates.

So no more lessons.
But I was actually *trying* –
and isn't that the thing about teaching –
you should
praise the effort,
not the result?

ZED
The thing about physics is,
if we input the correct data,
we should always
    be able to

plot^x a^x perfectly^x straight^x graph^x line^x

            & achieve

predictable | RESULTS |

However,
the look on my mother's face
    when I tell her about tonight's party
    informs me that –
    despite her consistent maternal programming –
    this is an entirely unexpected outcome.

She insists on driving me
    & picking me up
    afterwards.

MARNIE

Are you sure you've got a lift home?
Mum asks. *The buses stop at ten.*

I roll my eyes and repeat the lie.
I said I had, with Zed.
I'll walk home if I have to.

*I'm so happy
you're making friends at last,*
Mum says.

She watches me
painting a self-portrait
on the canvas of my face.
Her own is scrubbed bare because
she's on night-shift cover,
doing overtime for extra ££££.

And, just in case –
she hesitates a second
then pulls out her purse –
maybe you should take

I fumble the catch
and the shiny foil square
skids to a stop
by my foot.

MUM!!!!!
I wait till her cackles of laughter fade
before slipping it
safely
into my purse.

Harry lives at the posh end of town.
Under the street lights, the parked-up SUVs sparkle,
so clean you could lick their bonnets.

Two girls in strappy
stiletto heels
totter past,
holding bottles.
They stop outside a house
lit up like a Halloween pumpkin.

The mouth of the pumpkin opens,
belching a blast of noise,
and swallows them up.

I clutch my bottle of cider
closer to my chest.

Here goes.

Chapter
Eleven

ZED
After approximately one nanosecond
    in Harry Borman's house
I know for absolute certain
    that parties will
    never be my
    thing.

The hallway is already a
    sweaty press of bodies
    & it's only nine o'clock.
The air is so . . . *moist*.
    I'm inhaling a repulsive mix of sweat &
        fat white vape-clouds.

Music pumps out from the living room,
    annoyingly, ear-shatteringly,
    bouncily, depressingly, *upbeat*.
Too loud for me to think.

Just as I predicted, people are dancing.
There are strobe lights & I hope
    no epileptic guests.

I locate the toilet.

MARNIE
It's rocking in here!
I set off down a fogged-up hallway,
    hoping to find a drink.

ZED
When I emerge,
I spot Marnie heading down the hall
   inhaling from her plastic poison stick.
So much for trying to quit.

I look around for Luca.

MARNIE
I spot Zed looking like a lost child.
He must be hot
in that zipped-up tracksuit.

I'm already regretting my polo neck.
Sweat prickles as it trickles
between my boobs.

In the kitchen, a crowd is dipping mugs
into a plastic bowl. I dip too.
The liquid's red:
it tastes like wine
but only
sort of.

Zed is helping himself to milk
from the fridge.
Unbelievable.

Hi, Marnie!
It's the boy with the fade from my form.
Omar, I think.

Wow! Cool outfit.
He strokes the sleeve of the biker jacket
that wasn't so big on Dad.

> *You can drop this in the cloakroom.*
> *First door on the left.*
> He points to the hallway.

ZED
I can't see Luca.
Harry Borman swaggers past & says,
Oh my life, look what turned up!
I get a few double takes,
    people nudging each other in
    tacit surprise,
but none of them
    comes to talk to me.
Am I supposed to just
    break into a group?

Nobody else is
    wearing a tracksuit.

I lean against the cooker &
    accidentally turn the gas on
    with my buttock.

The Bunsen-burner smell
    lingers like flatulence
    until I flap it away,
spilling Omar's drink,
but he doesn't notice.

MARNIE
When I come back to the kitchen,
Harry Borman's standing in a corner,
not wearing Jessica, I note.
He waves at me to come over.

Adrenaline spikes a shiver
down my leg. *Game on.*

ZED
By the fridge,
Marnie is laughing at something
   Harry Borman said.
Her cheeks are flushed.
Perhaps I should look elsewhere
   for Luca.

MARNIE
The kitchen empties. Harry and I stay.
We refill our mugs from
the Punchbowl of Doom.
Harry says it's an 'everything' cocktail.
Essentially it saves time.

Gets the job done quicker!
He grins and knocks it back in one.

I like a fast worker, I say,
making my *double entendre* quite clear.

Harry's eyes check me out,
sweeping like a body scanner.
I like your boots, he says,
looking at my boobs.
They're awesome.

I like yours too, I say,
staring at his tight T-shirt,
at a six-pack ridged
as hard as ribs.

Someone ups the volume.
Beyoncé thumps through the wall
like she's trying to break it down.

We have another drink.

ZED
Where is he?
I check the living room,
weaving my way through the
    heaving tangles, muttering
    Excuse me . . . excuse me . . .

The L-shaped sofa is draped in bodies
    talking & drinking & kissing.

The strobing comes from a
    phone screen, throbbing
    face up on a coffee table.
Jessica & her coven dance in its light,
    pulsing unpleasantly.

No Luca.

MARNIE
No Jessica? **I yell, trying not**
to spray him with my spit.

Harry jerks a thumb sideways.
She's dancing. We're on a break. Again.

We drink some more.

ZED
Luca invited me.
He's got to be here, surely.
I pretend to examine a bookshelf.

MARNIE
There's no doubt about it,
Harry's hitting on me.

When he hands me my next
brimming cup,
he trails
the very tip of his finger
along my forearm
and all the little hairs
stand up in salute.

I wanted to channel chill,
but my cheeks are heating up
like charcoal.

My heart's *crazy-jumping. God, I'm boiling, I've got to get out of this jumper but I've only got a bra on underneath, I bet my face is bright red and what about him and Jessica, have they actually* split up?

My fingers stretch out
to touch Harry's chest.
His eyes widen.

Jessica! he yelps,
and I swing round.

Jessica's standing,
plastic pint glass in hand,
staring at me.
She's wearing a minidress glittering with scales,
as tight-fitting as snakeskin.

YOU SLUT!

Her voice cracks over the music
like sniper fire.
Get away from my boyfriend!

A flash of her hand and
I'm blinking her drink
out of my eyes.

ZED
There is shouting:
from Jessica Bates, if I'm not mistaken.
The front door slams.

Zed! There you are!
It's Luca, coming in from the garden.
So good you've finally come out!
He reaches across me to
 grab a half-full glass from the bookshelf,
drains it & smiles at me –
 encouragingly,
  expectantly.

Have I?

Have I *come out?*
Is that what I've done?

Luca begins to sway
    his hips in a figure of eight,
    his long arms doing something else
    quite complicated.

He beckons for me to follow.
I shake my head. *I can't dance.*

He laughs & shouts in my ear,
Everyone can dance!
Just close your eyes & feel the music,
let the beat take your body.

He waves his arms in the air.
Lose your inhibitions!
Move like no one's watching!
Nobody will laugh at you,
I promise.

I look around. Everyone else is dancing.
It's *me* who is the oddity, standing still.
Surely it's only a matter of synchronisation?
I listen to the beat & do as I'm told,
    keeping my eyes tight shut.

Sway, sway, *swing.*
Sway, sway, *swing.*
I'm getting the hang of it now, I think . . .
It's definitely easier when I can't see other people.

Sway, sway, *swing.*
Sway, sway, *swing,* jiggle, bounce –
There is clapping.

Am I getting applause?
Sway, sway, *swing*, jiggle, bounce –

MARNIE
Harry's apologising,
mopping me up like
a spilled drink.

My jumper's soaked.
He says come upstairs,
he'll sort me out
with a T-shirt.

As we pass the living room,
I hear clapping and take a look.

Surrounded by cheering, jeering, clapping, papping partygoers.

Zed's
dancing
like it's 1973.

It's too late to help him now.

I stumble
up the stairs
after Harry.

ZED
Like a lifeguard,
Luca fishes me out from the laughter.
He's laughing too –
    but not unkindly.
Okay, I take it back!
He smooths his fringe out of his eyes.
Maybe dancing's not for everyone.

I can feel my face strobing.

Let me grab us a drink, he says.
We'll go in the garden.
Don't worry about all that lot –
he jerks a thumb at the unkind crowd.
    They'll get over it.

Harry's garden is the size of a small park,
strung with fairy lights &
    dotted with dark corners.
Bottles float in a fish pond,
    keeping cool.
We sit in the shadow of a shrub.

I can't think of anything else to say.
But when Luca leans towards me,
I understand that
    chit-chat
    is not required.

MARNIE
Along the floor of Harry's bedroom
a row of dumbbell weights line up
obediently.

Harry's swearing about Jessica,
rummaging in a drawer
for a top that will fit me,
chucking a pile of clothes on the bed.

I agree that Jessica doesn't own him, that
she was bang out of order.

Then,
slowly,
swaying slightly
as it goes over my head,
I *p-e-e-l* off that sodden
and suffocating jumper,
and let Harry have
an eyeful.

ZED
I really like you.
Luca closes his eyes,
    parts his lips &
    moves closer
    as though my mouth is a magnet,
an opposite pole
    to which he is irresistibly attracted.

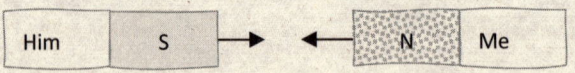

Our lips touch.

As though his mouth is a magnet
    to which I'm utterly repelled,
    I recoil at the strangeness of
    another person's lips against mine.

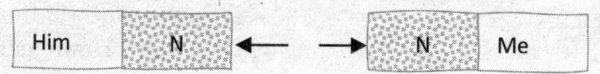

Panic squeezes my chest.
I jerk away.

Oh hey! I'm sorry!
Luca's eyes fly open.
Tiny rainbow fairy lights
    dance across each dark iris.

Too close. He's too close. He's much too close.

I scramble to my feet. Luca does too.
We stand, poles apart.

I thought you liked me? he says.

He's still in my face. I take a step back.
I did! I mean – I do – but –

What I really didn't like was
    what we just did.

Kissing, it turns out,
is not my thing either.

My face feels mugged.

MARNIE
Downstairs,
the beat has changed
to a throbbing pulse.

Harry cups my B cup.
Pulls off his T-shirt.

Downstairs,
my beat has also changed
to a throbbing pulse.

ZED
I'm sorry, Luca says again,
　　if I read your signals wrong, I –

I back away from him.

I think . . . I say –
　　because I don't know
　　how to say what I'm thinking –
I think I'll go home now.

MARNIE
Harry turns away to
put on music,
something cheesy
that syncopates uneasily
with the beats downstairs.

Actually I'm feeling a bit sick.
I try breathing slowly
in
out
but there isn't enough air.

I love this track, Harry says, coming back.
Do you like it?

Uh-huh, I mumble,
though actually, not much.

He stops my mouth with kisses.

I am being slow-danced backwards
towards a bed humped high
with tangled tops.

Harry does a *Strictly* swoop and
scoops out an arm.
The clothes cascade to the carpet.

In a badly balanced back-bend dip,
I tip and trip and hit the mattress.
He throws himself on top
and somehow we are both
lying on his bed.

I close my eyes and wish
the walls would stop
waltzing.

When I open them again, I'm still dizzy.
Staring at the bright light bulb,
my head swirls.

You are gorgeous, Harry is saying,
I love your hair loose like this.
He drapes it over my face like a blindfold.
I listen to my modesty being
unzippppped.

I'm shedding more inhibitions
with every piece of clothing.
This is it, I think.
It's happening.

I fumble
awkwardly for my purse,
and hold it out to Harry.
There's a condom in the pocket.

He laughs.
Gets up and switches off the light.

Did you find it? I ask.

Don't worry, babe,
says his voice in the sudden dark,
I got this covered.

. . . . I lie back and let Harry
take control.

ZED
I want to leave *now*.

I sit at the bottom of the stairs
& text my mother for pick-up.

Omar is on the step above me.
I turn my face to the wall
   to avoid eye contact,
but there's something he wants to share.

Oh, man! he says. *Did you HEAR?*
Jessica drink-slapped Marnie!
That mad cow threw, like, a whole pint in her face!
Marnie's still getting changed upstairs.

I hesitate, mid-text. Poor Marnie.
Perhaps I should offer a lift.

I decide to wait on the stairs for her.
In the next room, the music has changed
   to something that batters my skull.

Hurry up, Marnie.

MARNIE
On top of me
Harry's speeding up
like he's in a hurry.

The queasy orange street light
sends stripes across
his freckled shoulders.

Above him,
a familiar
cigar-smoking,
muscle-bound,
woman-hating,
millionaire hustler
stares straight-mouthed
from a poster on the wall.

I look into the eyes
of this false god,
this horrifying hero
of a thousand stupid
boy-dreams,
and suddenly I'm sober
& everything is wrong.

What am I doing?
What am I doing?
What am I doing?

I've changed my mind.
I've made a mistake.
I need him to stop.

But the rhythm of his breath
is hot against my ear and
how can I say I've changed my mind
now?

But I have to, I have to, I have to –

STOP!

                              And to my surprise,
                                      he does.

ZED
Marnie comes stumbling
    down the stairs, big
    boots clutched in her hand.

She's still in her black jumper.
Harry stands watching her go, hands on hips,
also a little dishevelled.

I say, *Marnie . . . ?*
    but she ignores me &
    pushes past unsteadily,
    bouncing a bit off the banisters.

Harry says curtly,
    You'd better take her home.
She's out of it.

He steps back & shuts the door.

In the front garden
Marnie glugs wine like Ribena.
I suggest she desists
& she tells me where I can go.

Fortunately my mother arrives promptly.
None of us speaks the whole journey home:
I am grateful not to discuss
    the evening's disasters.

Mother is silent even when
Marnie makes sick-noises
    & sticks her head out of
    the window.

I breathe through my mouth
    the rest of the way.

Chapter Twelve

MAR*skewering* NIE
It must be morning.
The sun is skewering my eyeballs
through a chink in the curtains
What happened last night?

I don't remember coming home
but here I am in my bed with
puke-smelling hair,
my party clothes
puddled on the floor.

I hug the duvet around my ears
and close my eyes
against the light.

Behind my lids,
memories
flash
like a
recap
montage.

Harry's mouth on mine
his voice in my ear,
his hands on my body,
his –
oh!
an image
like a cosh
that crashes
against my skull.

He put it in, didn't he?
At least for a little bit.

I touch the slight soreness
between my legs.

That little bit
was all it took
to change my state.

I've given away
my virginity
to someone else's boyfriend.

I'm such an idiot.

I must have slipped to sleep again
because realisation
is a rough hand
shaking me awake.

What have I done?

My bag's on the floor.
I open it with a gunshot snap
and scrabble through the mess.
To my relief,
the condom isn't there, it's okay.
There's only a wad of sick-stinky tissue.

Thanks, Mum,
I guess.

I stagger to the loo
to flush the soggy mess away
and hunt the paracetamol.

On top of the
bathroom cabinet
my fingertips brush up
against mum's stash
of emergency contraception.
I guess she doesn't mess up much,
judging by the blanket of sticky dust
so thick
I can lift it like cotton wool.
Maybe, just in case, I should –

But Mum's thundering up the stairs,
so I dash back to my bedroom.

She stands blocking my doorway
with her fists digging dips
in the flesh of her hips.

Awake, are we?
She scowls. *Last night
your friend's mum rang me at work
and said I had to come home
to look after my drunken daughter!*

You didn't have to.
The carpet is rolling under my feet,
I hang on to my desk to keep upright.

*What, and leave you
to choke on your own sick?*

Not a good look
for a nurse, I guess.

Well, missy, you can get yourself dressed
and clean up the mess you made.
You threw up in Mrs Donovan's car, remember?

No, I don't.
I can't even remember
what Zed's mother looks like,
let alone the car.

Mum throws a pair of jeans in my direction.
No arguing, Marnie.
Get dressed.
I'm driving you over.

ZED
I wake up at nearly midday,
   annoyed at myself for
   missing my planned revision slot.
But when I enter the kitchen,
   lunch isn't even started.
Mother appears to be in her study working
   again, even though it's a Sunday.
Perhaps that's just as well.
She was furious about the car.

The doorbell rings & it's Marnie
   standing shivering on the doorstep.
Morning! she mutters.

It's the afternoon
   & you look dreadful.
Her skin is green-tinged,
   her eyes bruised blue by last night's make-up.

She shrugs. *Thanks.*
I've come to clean the car.

Good, I say,
& hand over the equipment
    Mother left out for me:
- bucket
- car shampoo
- rubber gloves
- wellington boots
- knee-length apron

I direct her to the outside tap.

Marnie pulls a face
but scrubs in silence at the car
    until the last trace of her DNA is gone.

Even when she's done
    we still don't talk about
    what happened at the party.

She leaves.

MARNIE
I can't get away fast enough.
I leg it down Zed's drive
clutching my condom, the one
I found in the footwell of the car,
its wrapper unripped,
perfectly intact –
unlike me.

I remember Harry's voice in the sudden dark.
Don't worry, babe, I got this covered.

But if he used a condom,
it certainly wasn't mine.

I count the days of my cycle and
I'm bang in the middle.
Of course I am.

I run all the way home,
feeling sick at the dull
thud of my footsteps
sledgehammering my skull.

It's already the afternoon -
will Mum's morning after pill still work
if it's *after* the morning after?

Marnie? Mum calls out
as I run past the kitchen
and take the stairs
two at a time.
Marnie?

I lock the bathroom door
and try to open the packet
without disturbing the dust.
My fingers are sweaty.
Am I too late?

I squint at the packet.
I don't know why
they call it the *morning after* pill,
because even through a film of grey
it clearly says
you can take it
up to five days after.

                              Phew!
                           I pop out
                         the single pill
                      and slide the pack back
                       so it looks untouched.

                          Mum yells, *Marnie!*
                       Have you got homework?

                            I swallow it quick.

ZED
I can't work it out.
I'm expecting another lecture about the friends I keep, but
Mother hardly checks the car.

At supper she is
    distracted by her phone,
    not normally permitted at the table.

It all adds to my anxiety
    about school tomorrow.

How can I face my classmates
    after the humiliation of my dancing?

How can I face Luca
    after the horror of that kiss?

MARNIE
On Monday I have to face
not only the twin hurdles of
Jessica and Harry,
but a whole school
jumping with gossip.

Rakel rugby-tackles me before I even get
through the doors of reception.
*Marnie! Is it true Jessica Bates glassed you
cos you were talking to Harry?*
She sounds excited,
like she hopes it really happened.

Do I look glassed?
I tip my chin to the jaunty angle
I plan to keep it at today,
come what may.

Rakel reports the juiciest rumours:

Jessica glassed me and I went to A & E.
I pulled out her hair extensions.
Zed made a complete tit of himself.
Harry and Jessica have made up.

It turns out that
two of these are actually true.

I will get through this day
by keeping a Teflon smile
plastered across my face.

ZED
Today is not a good day.
Ms Rahman has given her permission
for me to wear my headphones
except when her mouth is moving.

I might be the class joke
but I just want to concentrate on
    my open books,
       on next week's Marathon.

I want to be
    as invisible as
        dark matter.

I want to pretend
    the party never happened.

MARNIE
Zed arrived with his head down,
hermetically sealed inside his
headphones.

I hope he didn't hear
the slow handclap
welcoming him in.

ZED
During registration
Marnie slips me a note.
She's drawn a girl
    in a miniskirt
    dancing with
    a boy with long hair
    & a tracksuit.

Next time,
    she whispers,
    we'll show those sad-asses
    how it's really done.

MARNIE
Zed smiles at the drawing
but he still looks like
his batteries
have died.

ZED
At break time Luca ambushes me
as I hide by the bike sheds.

Look, I'm sorry! he says. *I got it wrong.*
But why can't we just
   carry on
   like it didn't happen?
I thought you fancied me –
   but you don't. No biggie.

He puts his hand on my arm.
I flinch. He removes it hastily.

Relax! he says. *It's not that deep.*

Not for him, maybe.

MARNIE
I've thought of another way to
cheer Zed up.

ZED
I'm standing in the lunch queue
when my phone buzzes with a text.
It's Marnie, who's actually
   standing right behind me.

MARNIE
Zed's still got his headphones on.
I message him, not even fingers-crossed.

> i'm giving up the vapes
> for real this time.
> promise!

Zed checks his phone and turns around.
Wow! When he smiles,
that boy's got amazing cheekbones.

ZED
I eat in comfortable silence
   while Marnie talks at me.
She refuses the real banana I offer
   to replace her fruit flavours.
You're all right, mate, she says.

Actually, I think I might be.

MARNIE
Spanish is tough.
Like the flirting and the friendship
   never happened,
Harry Borman's blanking me,
   acting as if I'm invisible.

He doesn't say a word till home time,
   when he leans across
   the desk and whispers,
      SLUT!
   so quietly
   only I can hear.

I stiffen
but otherwise
don't give a sign
I heard. Did I really
seriously fancy him?
Now all I can see
is how he leers
at Rakel, jeers
at Zed, hates
any kid who's
a bit different.
I should have
seen before that
Harry Borman
is basically a
total waste
of oxygen, no
better than a
walking knob,
just using me to
prove to Jessica
she'd better watch it
if she doesn't want to
lose him. I wonder if he
ever actually fancied me
at all or if the whole point
was just to boast that he
shagged that new girl
and she   was crap?

As I walk out the gate,
I pass the happy pair.
Jessica is stuck to Harry's face like
chewing gum under a desk.

They're so engrossed,
they miss the finger
I flip them.

Chapter Thirteen

ZED
It's a week after the party
    & like Luca promised,
    everyone's moved on.

I'm back on track,
    getting my feet into the starting blocks
    for the *Physics Marathon, Round One*.

As I enter the exam room,
The Doc pats my shoulder –
meaning, I presume, to reassure,
but it's actually very awkward.

I'm our school's solitary candidate –
which is fortunate
    since the only room free
    is the First Aid Suite, which is really
    an oversized cupboard.
To ensure I don't cheat
    The Doc will have to
    invigilate me through the window.

I cram my legs under the tiny desk.
Next to the sink, the handwashing notices
    are covered in case they give any clues,
& the defibrillator's blanketed –
but I'm glad it's close
    because my heart is beating
    three times faster,
    tachycardiac.

I've emptied my head onto the squares
    of the answer sheet,
    ciphered my thoughts into calculations & graphs.

I wave at Dr Allinger through the glass.
He frowns & checks his watch.
There are
    fifteen minutes & twenty-two seconds
        of test time remaining,
but I'm definitely done.

I cap my pen with satisfaction.
Possibly a personal best.

MARNIE
Mr Challoner has made no comment
about my floral fannies.
I think he's embarrassed.

But Naomi is cool,
just out of art school
and sparking with ideas.

We talk about my *Freedom* project,
about what I could do with
screen prints and typesetting and linocuts and videos and
murals and installations and soundscapes and sculpture
and wire-modelling and pastels and charcoal and clay and
oh! so many techniques
I never even knew
existed.

When I walk into the next art lesson,
Naomi's working on something.
Her hair's in puffs,
big fists bunching from her head,

She calls me over.

On the bench in front of her
lies a netted frame
like a small mosquito screen.

Watch this.
She opens a tin and
deftly spreads a streak of red ink across
the top of the frame,
then drags a squeegee
slowly down the patterned mesh

*in one
sure stroke.*

It's silk screen printing, she says.
*I found the equipment
covered with cobwebs
in the cupboard.*

The air's sharp with the stink of ink.
I watch as she reverses direction,
pushing the colour
to the top of the frame
again

What's the printing for? I ask.

Naomi's smile broadens
as she lifts the screen to reveal
a black-and-red poster.

*MY BODY
MY CHOICE!*
it says.

A fist
punches through
a gendered cross.

*I'm going on a march
at the weekend
to support
our sisters in the States.*
She clips
the wet poster
to the drying line
stretched overhead.
Do you like it?

I stare upwards.

Nothing else along that artistic laundry line, none of the

limp *landscapes* or *wishy-washy watercolours* or stale **STILL LIFES**

comes even *close* to the impact
of those bold words.

As I watch her clean the screen, I get an idea.
*Naomi, could I learn how to screen-print
for my final exam?*

She stops scraping ink back into the tub
and laughs.
I was sort of hoping you'd say that!

Maybe I could screen-print
my various varieties of vulva?
Like Andy Warhol's Monroes, maybe
I could print the same design

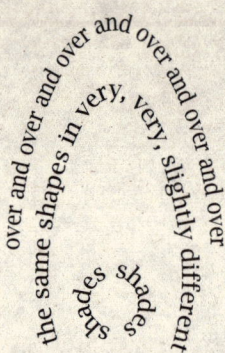

over and over and over and over and over and over and over the same shapes in very, very, slightly different shades shades shades

I'm sketching out a plan when
Naomi peers over my shoulder.
*Why not
make FREEDOM
more personal?* she suggests.
You've still got time.

*You can't get much more personal
than private parts!*
I protest.

Naomi laughs. *Express your own ideas,*
she says. *Don't ape Warhol and O'Keeffe.
For example, my poster –
it's about what freedom means to **me** . . .*
She hesitates, then undoes her apron.
Look . . .

BLACK LIVES MATTER
declares her T-shirt.

For me, she says quietly,
*it's also freedom from harassment.
From stop and search. From prejudice . . .*

She covers the slogan back up
before Mr Challoner sees.
*But freedom means something
different for everyone, right?
It all depends whose foot is on your neck.*

She gets up off the stool.
I'll let you think about it.

I stare at the bench.

In truth
all those vulvas
were getting a little vanilla.

My idea of freedom?
What do I want to be free from?

My brain starts whirring
like Naomi's words have wound me up.

She's lit a touchpaper inside my head
and I swear rockets are going off – it's like
Fireworks Night in there.

Naomi smiles at the look on my face.
That's it, Marnie. Show us what's inside that rebel head.

I fill page after page *page after page after page after page after page after page after page after page after* of a new sketchbook.

Me and Rakel and Luca and Zed
have started hanging out.

Four lunch trays squaring up together forming a fortress every lunchtime.

Even Jessica Bates
can't penetrate
this Roman shield
formation.

ZED
People are like unstable atoms,
so anxious to group together,
to form bonds.

This has never affected me before,
but perhaps Marnie
    has provided the catalyst,
because I appear to have
    bonded.

MARNIE
Harry and Jessica spend every break time
with their tongues rammed
down each other's
throats.

They're welcome to each other,
but it does make me
feel a bit
sick.

ZED
My Spanish accent continues to resist
    Marnie's coaching.
She says I sound like a
    cat being slowly strangled.

I try to clear my throat of cats, but to no avail.
Finally, Marnie says there is *nada* more
    she can do for me.

We focus on physics instead.

MARNIE
If Zed was an artist, not a physicist,
he'd probably be Dalí.
Physics is surreal.

ZED
It occurs to me
   Marnie may be interested
   in the philosophy of physics.
Have you ever heard of Schrödinger
& his famous cat experiment? I ask.

                              MARNIE
                              Oh, kill me now.
                              An actual cat? I ask,
                              opening my eyes
                              as wide as they'll go.

ZED
Or a wolf, or a tiger.
It's irrelevant.
He shut it in a cardboard box —

                              MARNIE
                              A tiger in a cardboard box?
                                      No! Get real.

ZED
It wasn't.
Real, I mean.

                              MARNIE
                              Don't care.
                              You can't keep a
                              tiger in a cardboard box –
                              or a wolf, for that matter –

ZED
Shhh, listen!
I wave an impatient hand.
Marnie's concern is
    completely misplaced.
*This was a theoretical experiment
    to test the notion of a quantum state.
He put poison in the box –*

                        MARNIE
                        That's animal abuse!
                        I clutch Zed's arm.
                        He pointedly prises
                        my fingers away.

ZED
I'm beginning to think
Marnie is deliberately
    missing the point.
*It's radiation.
There's a Geiger counter which –*

                        MARNIE
                        I interrupt.
                        Somebody should report him!

ZED
I give up.

MARNIE
Zed gives up
trying to tell me
what I actually already know,
which is that nobody knows
if the cat is dead or alive
until they open the box.

(Spoiler: until they open the box
the cat is both dead **and** alive.)

Whatever, I say.
Poor cat.

Zed rolls his eyes.

ZED
*Marnie, I promise you,
it's not actually
   about the cat.*

MARNIE
It's such fun
to press his buttons.

ZED
Marnie walks away, laughing.

Later in the library
my head is down, white noise is playing.

From the corner of my eye
I detect Luca stalking me –
creeping like an outsized
very-much-alive cat
towards my table.

BOO!
Luca lifts my earphones off my head,
& listens to the sound of static.
Awesome playlist, dude.
He smiles at me, an easy grin.

Luca always acts as though
    the party never happened,
but I can't blank it out.

My dancing may no longer be legend,
    but I won't forget
    that failure of a kiss.

Want to hang out after school? he asks now.
As mates? No strings attached.

I say I'll think about it.

MARNIE
Mr Challoner's making us all
practise for the *Living Objects*
GCSE project theme
even though,
since I'm doing *Freedom*,
it's a waste of my time
and
an infringement on my
artistic liberty.

He brought in a
a crate of apples to draw,
wrinkled and close to death.
I bet Naomi would at least have chosen
something more exciting,
like mangoes.

Right now,
she's talking to me quietly
as I sweep charcoal across the page,
and it's hard to keep my hand steady
as her words paint a picture of a future
I didn't know could be mine.

She says I've got such talent,
maybe I should consider
specialising *now*
instead of marking time
with two other A levels I don't want.

You don't have to make up your mind
straight away, she says.
Just have a think about it.

She hands me the
sixth-form college prospectus.
Here's all the info.
Talk it over with your mum.

My mum?
I stuff it in my bag without much hope.
We'll see how that conversation goes.

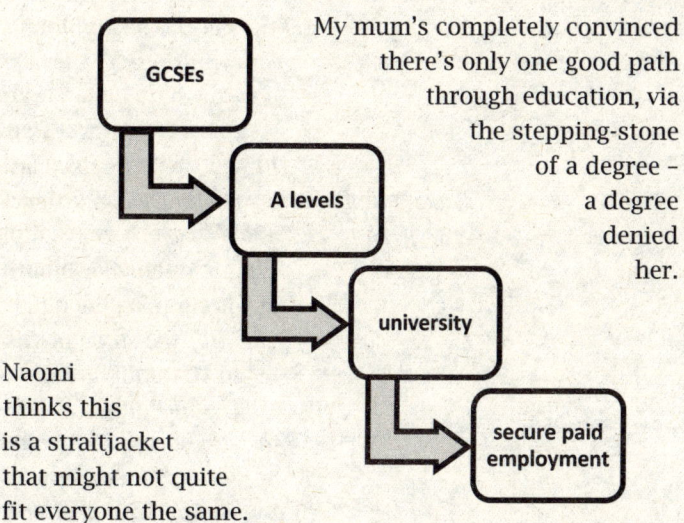

My mum's completely convinced
there's only one good path
through education, via
the stepping-stone
of a degree –
a degree
denied
her.

Naomi
thinks this
is a straitjacket
that might not quite
fit everyone the same.

The thing is, when you're
in a *one-parent* family,
you're in a *one-opinion*
family too.

Mum's opinion.

That night I wait till she's got a
mouthful of macaroni, then say casually
(like my whole future isn't riding on her response)
Mum, Naomi showed me
this art course for next year.
It's at a college near here and –

Whoa! Mum's fork clatters onto her plate.
She swallows hard.
Let me get this straight now.
You want to skip A levels?

Not skip!
I knew she'd be like this.
Take a diploma in Art and Design instead.

Mum opens her mouth
but I jump in again, quick.
It's the same points,
so I'd qualify for uni –
if *I decide to go –*
but I'll be doing something
I really enjoy!
It's a vocational qualification.
VOCATION. Like nursing, right?

Vocation is from the Latin word *vocatio*,
which means a call, a summons.
Mum's a nurse; she should get it.

I'm totally, completely, *utterly*
drawn to this.
She has to let me go.

The cheesy mac congeals on our plates
while I show her the prospectus, tell her about
the incredible facilities, all the things I could do,
all the jobs this could lead to
without drowning myself in debt.

Please, Mum! I'll work really hard!
I swear I won't kick off at college!
There'll be nothing to rebel against, will there?

Mum says nothing for the longest time.

I watch her brain
chase her heart
round her face,
and I brace.

Chapter Fourteen

ZED
I'm still waiting for the result
    of the Marathon trial.
I'm reasonably confident I got through, but
    it is theoretically possible
I made an error.

The longer I wait,
the less certain I become.

MARNIE
Mum makes me wait so long.
    She's thinking about it,
        she says.

I don't get an answer
until the next day, when she's back
from blowing this month's salary
on only the bare essentials.

She dumps a bag of bathroom stuff
    then smiles at me
    and says,
    Okay!

Mum! I love you!
I throw my arms around her
and she *oof!*s.

Of course, being Mum,
it's an *Okay* with strings attached.

Mum says dreams are like balloons.
They're fun to have,
but you've got to hold them tight
and keep your feet firmly
on the ground.

My mum is really clever. She wanted to become a doctor, but her dream balloon was popped when she got pregnant with me.

Maybe
she could still
have become a doctor
if my dad had done his share.

Mum insists
I can only study art at college
if I get what she calls some *insurance* –
results that will get me a job
if the art thing doesn't.

She says I have to get
grade six or more
in all the core
subjects.

Six? Easy! I say –
completely disregarding
how crap I am
at physics.

I head upstairs,
swinging a bag
of bathroom stuff.

But my bubble of joy deflates
when I tuck away
Mum's tampons.

Physics isn't all I've overlooked.
Shouldn't I have got
my period by now?

> **On day 32 of my cycle**
> I'm still waiting.
> Where's my bloody period?
>
> **By day 34**
> I'm properly worried. I'm not normally late.
> I'm dashing to the loo between lessons,
> but my gusset stays stubbornly spotless.
> Rakel thinks I've got the squits.

ZED

The results should be in this week.
I keep checking my pigeonhole
but there's nothing from The Doc.

MARNIE

> **Day 35 and**
> Luca and Rakel keep asking me if I'm okay.
> I'm beginning to think I'm really not.
>
> During an emergency appointment
> with Doctor Google, I think of asking
> a different question.

✦ AI Overview

Yes, taking the morning after pill can cause your period to be late, sometimes by up to a week, as it can interfere with ovulation and disrupt your menstrual cycle; if your period is significantly late after taking the morning after pill, it's advisable to take a pregnancy test and consult a healthcare professional.

               Phew. I feel
        my dream-balloon reinflate.

              Better still, that evening
         there's a tangible tinge on the toilet roll.
              An unmistakable streak.
              I could cry with relief.

ZED
The results are in. I'm through to the final!
I read Dr Allinger's email alone
    over a solitary supper of scrambled eggs
    since Mother's working late again.

He's extremely pleased – as am I.
I wasn't wrong about how well it went.
Ninety-four per cent correct.
At my calculation
    that puts me in the highest half-centile
    of the population.

I quell my slight annoyance
    that I dropped six marks,
& message Marnie the news.

                    ## MARNIE
                 Apparently, I have
           the brainiest friend on the planet.
                 All this good news
           definitely calls for a celebration.
             I send a couple of messages.

ZED
The doorbell app
   dingdongs on my phone.
I check the screen –
   but all I can see is a jiggle of scarlet.

MARNIE
Party-time!
I bought a bunch of balloons
as red as blood, since this is my
   secret celebration too.

ZED
It's no secret that
Marnie isn't exactly
   Mother's favourite person, so
   when I tap at the study door
   to check it's okay to have friends round,
I'm not expecting a
   Yes.

But in fact,
   all she says through the closed door is,
   Just keep the noise down,
   would you, please?
   I've got a lot of work on.

I cannot predict her
these days.

MARNIE
We talk quietly in
Zed's huge kitchen,
which is so spotless I wouldn't
dare open a can of beans.

Unlike my house,
you can't tell by smell
what they had for tea –
unless it was bleach.

Our floor's always sticky
with the footprints of food,
but Zed's tiles are gleaming clean.

He fetches milkshake from the
shipping container of a fridge
and I glimpse neatly ordered shelves.

Everything's very . . . sterile.

Rakel arrives with slabs of sticky,
nutty sweets to share, then Luca –
who doesn't bother with the doorbell.

He honks the rubber horn of his Chopper bike,
its frame glowing red with dozens of
solar-powered, chilli-pepper lights.

TA DA DA DA DA DA-DA!

> Zed's dragon of a mother
> comes roaring from her lair.
>
> No wonder poor Zed
> has issues.

ZED
We go to my room & close the door.
We eat sweets & drink milkshakes
    sitting on the floor.
They throw jelly babies at me
    when I suggest we play Monopoly.
I pretend I was joking.

Luca sets some music playing low
    & drops down next to me.
Relax! he says. *You're safe this time.*
I shift over a bit so our thighs don't touch.
I am *almost* okay with this.

He hands me a rainbow-coloured flyer.
It's from the local LGBTQ+ teen group.
They have a 'hangout' every second Saturday,
he says softly. *Want to come?*

I look up. Rakel & Marnie are on my bed
comparing the respective
    hairiness of their legs,
not listening.

I don't really think it's for me, I say quietly.
*I don't think I'm the
   hanging-out kind.*
I point to the poster,
the lengthy acronym.
Maybe this is not who I am?

Luca bursts out laughing.
Oh my lord! he whispers.
*You mean I kissed you
   & you're not even gay?
Man, I'm so sorry!*

I stare at my hands in my lap.
Don't be sorry. I– I–
Can I really be talking about this?
I don't know what I am.

Luca lets me change the subject.

MARNIE
Luca and Zed
are leaning their heads
together, talking in low voices.

Maybe it's just
to avoid the wrath of Dragon Mother,
but not for the first time
I wonder if there's
something
between
them.

Rakel says
I've got a dirty mind.

ZED
Would you mind leaving now?
My guests protest, but it's nearly eleven
    & I'm tired.
I've been making a lot of conversation.

I'll get up early tomorrow &
    do some more revision
    to compensate for the fun tonight.

In the hallway,
blue light still leaks from
    under Mother's study door.

Marnie & Rakel
    leave without a whisper,
    but Luca lingers.
He says maybe
    he just wasn't the right boy for me.

I look at that smile, the ridiculous fringe,
    those treacle eyes,
& I can't imagine who could
    possibly be righter.

But perhaps he's got a point:
maybe I should widen
    my sample size.

Luca threatens to

until I agree to hang out
with the *LGBTQ+ Teens*
tomorrow night.

He might be joking
    but I'm too exhausted to judge.

Chapter Fifteen

MARNIE
On Saturday I wake happy.
I swing my legs out of bed
and disturb a red balloon
which bobs along the floor,
reminding me.

I go to the loo.
That's odd.
There's still only
the faintest hint of pink
on the pad.

Back in bed,
I consult Doctor Google again.

✦ AI Overview

Yes, it is considered normal to experience a light period or spotting after taking the morning after pill, as the hormonal changes caused by the pill can often lead to irregular bleeding, including light periods or spotting between cycles; this usually isn't a cause for concern unless the bleeding is heavy or lasts longer than a few days.

Nothing to worry about then.
I just got off lightly
for once.

ZED
At supper on Saturday
I tell mother I have to
conduct an investigation
 with a friend.

Walking down the hill
    towards the youth club,
Luca is relaxed, but
    although the wind is chilly
    I'm sweating in my sweatshirt.
I wish I hadn't allowed
    him to convince me
    this was such a good idea.

I guess tonight is a biology
    experiment.
Am I or aren't I?
Am I or aren't I . . . *what?*

The youth club
    is in a disused church,
its entrance is swathed for the night
    in strings of rainbow bunting.

Luca smiles reassuringly as he opens the door.
They're a really nice crowd!
My heart syncs with the beat
    banging on the stained-glass windows.

MARNIE

Mum opens the door and she sniffs the air.
Let me guess – lasagne? Bless you! She hugs me,
post-shift tiredness and hospital stink
in every wrinkle of her tunic.
I hope it's ready – I'm starving!

I take off my apron with pride.
It feels good to give her
a *nice* surprise
for once.

ZED
It's time to go. I've had enough.
The lights are too bright, the music too loud,
& the adults are patronising.
Worst of all, dozens of queer teenagers are acting
    like I'm a steak
        thrown into a shark tank.

I signal Luca, frantically rolling my eyes
    towards the exit. I've got enough
    significant data.

We leave.

Outside, Luca slings an arm
    around me. *No good, huh?*
Never mind. Well done for trying.

Before I can pull away, a honking, screeching
    gaggle of girls
sways towards us from the bus stop.
One bright blonde head shrieks,
Aw, look – baby gays!

Please don't tell me that was Jessica Bates.

Chill, chill, chill, amigo!
Luca's panting because
I'm walking very fast up the hill.
It's blowing at least a force six.

Stop! Please, Zed!
He reaches out a hand but I speed up.
All right! he calls. *It was a mistake!*
Sorry! ¡Lo siento!

But I'm not angry with him.
I'm angry with *myself*.
   I just made the kind of repeated
            systematic
                  human error
                        I despise in others.

I'm not like other people.
Why did I have to prove it to myself
   all over again?
Now I'll have Jessica Bates to deal with.

Why? I snap over my shoulder. *Why should I
have to prove to anyone*
   what I am,
   or
   what I'm not?

I halt. That's it.
Luca bashes into me.

That's it!
The error is not with the experiment.
The mistake is not with me.
The flaw is with the whole *hypothesis*.

We all assume
   that everyone's got to be **something.**
We all have to be neatly boxed, with tags
   to define us:

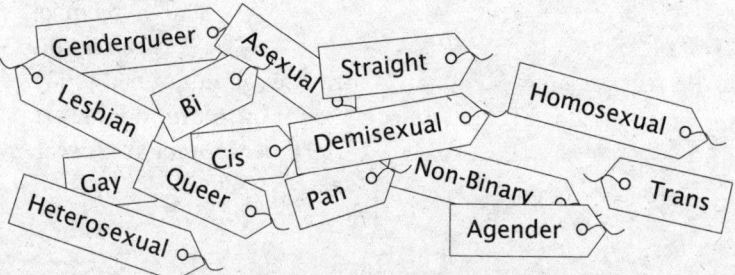

But what if none of those tags
    applies to me?
What if I am neither

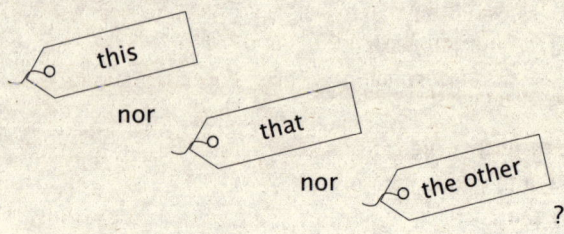

I turn to look Luca
    straight in the eye.
I don't think I'm anything.
If it makes people uncomfortable
    because they can't tick a box –
well, that's their problem,
not mine.

I set off again
    into the teeth of the biting wind.
Behind me, Luca shouts,
Cool, Zed! I get it!

MARNIE
The next day, Mum stands over me
    with a cup of tea.

C'mon, sleepyhead! she says, smiling.
    You'll be late for school!

School, *schmool.*
    I can hardly
drag myself out of bed today.
If it wasn't for double art,
I'd be skipping it, I swear.

I feel ABSOLUTELY wiped.

I roll onto my front and –
Ow!
It's like I was punched in the chest.
I gingerly pull on
my one-and-only sports bra
to hold my aching boobs in place.

Luca fills me in on the
teenage hang-out horror show
as we Monday-morning-slow-trudge
up the path to school.
I'm *so* knackered.

Ahead of us, a bunch of
Year Seven midges
are swarming by the wall,
giggling at something.

I don't see the big deal, I tell him.
Let him be . . . whatever.
So he wants to be undefined?
That's fine.

The cloud of prepubescents
disperses at our approach.

Actually, I say,
warming to my theme,
d'you know what?
Everyone should let the guy ***be***.
Just leave him alone.

But it's too late.

                          Luca points to
           where the Year Sevens were gathered,
   at a scribble of fresh graffiti on the bricks.

               It must've been Jessica Bates.
               She texts the same disgusting
                  homophobic hate crime
                    all around the school.

                She makes me so sick
                      I feel like
                    I might actually
                         throw up.

ZED
Marnie & Luca wouldn't tell me the words
    they spent all break time erasing,
but nothing gets scrubbed off the internet,
    & people keep shoving it under my nose.

I wouldn't mind so much, but
    what I was described as doing
    is not
            actually
                  anatomically
                        possible.
Literally bollocks.

Luca says it's best to sit tight,
    say nothing. Just wait for them
    to find another target.
But it feels wrong to be wishing this spotlight

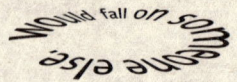
would fall on someone else

Chapter
Sixteen

ZED
It's been a week
& I'm still waiting
for their laughter
to stop hurting.

MARNIE
It's been a week
and I'm still waiting
for my boobs
to stop hurting.

It's lunchtime.
I sit on my own on a bench
by the art block,
with the wind snipping
through my too-thin coat.

Panic gnaws at my lungs.
I tell myself to breathe.
Be more Zed.
Think logically.
Look at the evidence,
the degree of certainty.

1. He was wearing his own condom (possibly).
2. He pulled out early (probably).
3. I took the morning after pill (definitely).
4. I had a period (sort of/maybe).

As Zed would say,
the potential to be pregnant is . . .
minimal?

I consult Doctor Google again.
He's not helpful.

✦ AI Overview

Sore breasts can be a side effect of taking a morning after pill, as it contains high levels of hormones that can cause similar symptoms to early pregnancy, including breast tenderness; however, the only way to confirm pregnancy is to take a pregnancy test, as many morning after pill side effects can mimic early pregnancy symptoms.

So I'm either pregnant
or I'm not?

FFS!
I could have told him that.

After that *Schrödinger*
of a diagnosis,
the next chance
to check my phone
is on the bus home.

I sit in the stink
of other people's chips
while the driver chucks us round
queasy-making bends.

I dig
deeper online,
shovelling through
all the small print that
I didn't read before.

I should have known
there'd be a get-out clause.

The manufacturers say that
no morning after pill
can be 100%
effective.

The bus brakes sharply on a corner
and throws me hard against the glass.

As Zed would say,
less than 100%
is a failure.

It gets worse, the more I read.
Apparently, if you've already ovulated,
the morning after pill
is 100%
INEFFECTIVE.

What the actual . . .?
The pill doesn't work
if you've already pinged out an egg?
How am I supposed to even *know?*
It's not like my ovaries
tag me in every time.

I check my planner, counting again
from my second day at Downham.
Like I thought, the party was
bang in the danger zone,
sixteen days into my cycle –
WHICH IS WHY I TOOK THE
FREAKIN' PILL
IN THE FIRST PLACE!

It makes as much sense
as paracetamol
not working
on an
actual headache.

I keep reading. It's unreal.
That very light period
I had?
It might not have been
a period at all –
just some hormonal hiccup.

I've been
shafted
by Big
Pharma.

That night I don't sleep.
I've got to know for certain,
I've got to know
one way
or
the other.

I've got to be brave.

I get up early.
Only one chemist is open before school,
but one chemist is all I need.

I don't know which test to get
until I see the prices.
Forget all the double packs,
one is all I can afford.

The assistant
wraps the box
discreetly and
eyes my uniform
like it's a dirty word.

At lunch and break time, I go to the toilets
with my shameful secret
disguised in a brown paper bag,
but Jessica or her cronies
are always clustered contouring
around the mirror,
and . . . just *no*.

But I've got to know.
I've just got to
be brave.

The last period is biology.
I'm sitting with Zed.
Mr Lawson says
we're supposed to be measuring
the speed of cell division,
and that's the
final straw.

I can't stand
being
pregnant
and
not pregnant
any longer,
not with the answer
right there in my bag.

Okay, Mr Schrödinger ...

I ignore the teacher's
Sit down, please!
and head for the door

... it's time to open the box.

ZED
Newton's third law states
   that for every action, every force in nature,
there is an equal & opposite
   reaction.

So when Marnie legs it out of class,
it's inevitable that Mr Lawson jumps to his feet.
Settle down, everyone!
These days though, very little Marnie does
   disturbs me, so I stay calm
   in my seat

waiting for a text of explanation
   that doesn't come.

MARNIE
Now all I have to do is wait.
I put the cap back on the pee-stick.

This could be the last
four minutes
of
life as I know it.

Four minutes.

Make the most of them, Marnie.
Listen to the thud-thud of my heart.
Smell the stink of the stalls.
Feel the wee spilled on my fingers.
See the seconds counting down
on my timer.

Three minutes.

I can't stand the suspense.
I need a distraction.
Rakel would pray,
but I don't believe in anything
except my own bad luck.

Two minutes.

I read the instructions again
and learn I should have done this
hours ago, with early-morning
concentrated urine.
If the result's negative
and my period still doesn't come,
I'll have to
find the money for another test
and go through it all again.

One minute.

I read the period-poverty sign
on the back of the cubicle door
seventeen times before
my eyes slide up.

Marnie is a slag
is scrawled across the top.

Jessica Bates is right to hate me.

I hate myself.

ZED
I get Marnie off detention
by lying to Mr Lawson
that she has *women's problems*,
& he goes an interesting
shade of red.

I text Marnie to say
not to worry, I got her off the hook,
But there's no reply. *Nada*.

She can thank me later.

MARNIE
My phone buzzes. *Time's up.*
I stab the button quiet
& swallow down sick.

I wish I wasn't here by myself.
I wish I'd told Zed.
I wish I wasn't feeling so

alone.

ZED
Class is over
    & still I'm on my own.
I look for Marnie, but she can't be found.

                    MARNIE
        But Zed would say, it won't go away
                just because you're
            pretending it's not there.

            Just do it, Marnie!
        says Zed's voice in my head.
            Just open your eyes
                  &
                    look.

👀

Chapter Seventeen

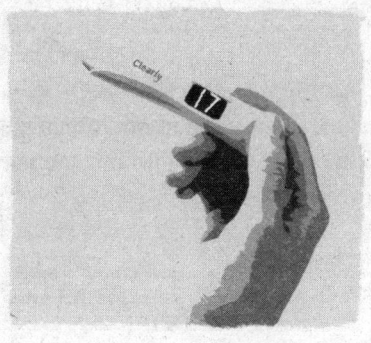

MARNIE
I blink.
turn it around
&
dn ʎɐʍ ɹǝɥʇo ǝɥʇ

Breathe in.
Breathe out.

Blink again.

But the two red lines are sti‖ there,
so strong
I feel
faint.

I'm not a teenager any more –
I'm a teenage *pregnancy*.
I'm a statistic.

The hooter goes.
Period seven's over now
and
I'm going home.

I think I've learned
all my lessons
for today.

Chapter
Eighteen

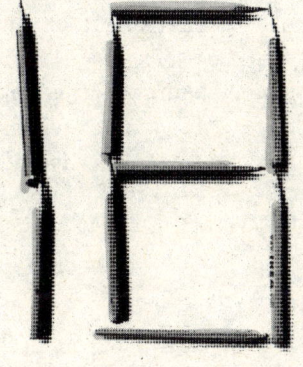

MARNIE
In the kitchen,
Mum's sniffing suspiciously
at a pack of ham.
Her frown deepens when she sees me.
Did you remember I'm on nights?
Bagels for tea – just cheese, I'm afraid.
Ham's off.

She doesn't like leaving me alone all night.

Of course, when I was at boarding school,
she didn't have to worry.
That's another thing I messed up.

Mum will leave for work at seven,
which suits me fine –
I only have to not-cry
until then.

I could eat my mattress
faster than I'm
getting through
this bagel.

Mum's going on about my application to college.
She uses the words *your future* a lot,
because she thinks
I still have one.

The brochure for the college lies
open on the table.

Cool, happy, sporty-looking students
stroll about the campus
clutching folders
(not baby-slings)
close to their chests.

A month ago
I could have been one of them,
but by September I'll be
the size of a house.

ZED

The house is quiet when I arrive home,
later than usual.
After school I trained for the Marathon
   with Dr Allinger, who said
   I'm in great shape.
Mother will be pleased.

I find her
still shut in her study.
I don't think she actually goes into
   the office much these days.

I knock & tell her   *through the door*   *Great*, she says,
   that Dr Allinger is   sounding like it's
   quietly confident I'll   anything but.
   make it to the
   finals.

But wasn't she the one
    who insisted this would
    clinch it for the
    super-selective sixth form?

I retire to my room
    in some confusion.

MARNIE
When Mum's gone
Doctor Google tells me
that at four weeks
my *zygote* is the
size of a poppy seed.

I wet my finger
and dab up the tiny dots
shaken to the table
from the
food-bank bun.

I'm amazed
and horrified that
that something so small
could mess me up
so

big.

That night I chase sleep,
    trying not to think
    about the stranger inside me –
    my little hitchhiker,
    my seed-sized stowaway.

The next morning I drag my weary body
    up the path to school
    with that stark stick of plastic
    stuck in my pencil case.

    I can't leave it at home,
    can't throw it away . . .

    Still can't quite believe it.

    Two parallel lines
    which = disaster.

    Rakel waves from the hockey pitch
    and I fake a smile back,
    my lips pressed tight
    on my secret.

If you believe any of the scrawl on this wall,
    Downham High is full of girls
    who do it
    all the time.

    Once.
    I've only ever done it *once.*
    Not even once really, not properly.

So why me?

Why me? Why me? Why me? Why me? Why me?
Why me? Why me? Why me? Why me? Why me?
Why me? Wh   hy me? Why me?
Why me?   me? Why me?   me? Why me?
Why m   hy me? Why me? Wh   ? Why me?
Why me? Why me? Why me? Why   ? Why me?
Why me? Why me? Why me? Why   ? Why me?
Why me? Why me? Why me? Why   ? Why me?
Why me? Why me? Why me? Why   ? Why me?
Why me? Why me? Why me? Why   e? Why me?
Why me? Why me? Why me? W   me? Why me?
Why me? Why me? Why me?   y me? Why me?
Why me? Why me? Why m   Why me? Why me?
Why me? Why me? Wh   ? Why me? Why me?
Why me? Why me?   me? Why me? Why me?
Why me? Why me? Why me? Why me? Why me?
Why me? Why me? Why me? Why me? Why me?
Why me? Why me? Why me? Why me? Why me?
Why me? Why me?   me? Why me? Why me?
Why me? Why me?   me? Why me? Why me?
Why me? Why me? Why me? Why me? Why me?
Why me? Why me? Why me? Why me? Why me?

ZED
No more about me on the wall today.
No new lies.
No fresh sordid speculations
    about what I might be doing with whom
    or the ways
    I might be doing it.

It looks as if
    Luca was right –
these storms blow over.

I walk into reception
wondering if today
    they've got
        another victim in their sights.

Marnie's in her place already,
staring into space.

Far from thanking me
    for my quick thinking in biology,
she's *blanking* me.
Blanking us all.

We sit through registration & PSHE
& she hardly says a word.

Luca's dark eye catches mine.
He jerks a thumb & mouths
What's up with her?

Marnie & my mother:
both mysteries.

MARNIE
I spend break time staring at Harry Borman,
wishing he'd choke on the crisps
he's stuffing down
his stupid throat.

But it's me who's choking.
Choking on the stupid lie
I swallowed.

Don't worry, babe. I got this covered.

How could he have lied about
something so important?

And worse –
how could I ever
have believed
him?

At lunchtime, he flashes
his phone at Rakel
and jeers, *These your tits?*

Then he starts a food fight,
yelling and shouting and throwing
half-eaten burger buns
across the room.

He squirts Zed's milk carton
right in Luca's face, taunting him.
This how you like it?

How could I have ever fancied
that utter moron?

Was I blind?

He's obscene and
obnoxious and a
waste of air
and I
can't believe
I let this boy
even *touch* me,
let alone . . .
let alone . . .
let alone . . .

I jump to my feet
and scream
as loudly as I can,

SCREW
YOU!

ZED
When Marnie leaps up & yells at Harry,
   her bag opens
                   &

scatters

            gel pens   pencil case

                    sketchbook

BOOKS   **BOOKS** *pencils*   highlighters

                BOOKS   BLOCK NOTEPAD
       pencils   **BOOKS**
                      rubbers   lip balm

all over the floor.

The on-duty teacher can't ignore
   this canteen Armageddon.
You, girl! he yells.
We will not have shouting
   in the dining room!
Outside, please, NOW!

Marnie storms out, stuffing
   half the known universe back into
   her bag.

Luca wipes the milk from his eyes, laughing.

Rakel's picking up some pens
   that Marnie must have missed.

What's this? she says,
looking at something small & white.
Her face goes funny.
She stuffs the something in her pocket
& hustles us out of the hall.

In a corner of the atrium,
Rakel holds it out.
Look, she says, *what Marnie dropped!*

Luca examines it closely.
Hang on! Isn't that a . . . ?

It is! breathes Rakel.
She looks at us open-mouthed.
Oh, Marnie!

I take the plastic stick from Luca.
Oh my goodness, yes.
It's clearly a test –
& it's clearly positive.
Two red lines.

I hold it at arm's length
   as though it were   radioactive
& fumble in my blazer
   for the face mask I always carry
   in case of contamination.

No wonder Marnie was out of sorts today.

You realise what this means? I ask.
We might be positive too!

Luca & Rakel look surprised.
I don't think they understand the
    implication for me.
I elucidate.
I could miss the Physics Marathon!

I'm aware I sound unsympathetic, but
Marnie really shouldn't be in school.

Covid is highly contagious.

Chapter
Nineteen

ZED
What?
Marnie's *pregnant*?

MARNIE
I'm wandering the corridors
when my phone buzzes.
I go cold with shock
when I see
a picture of a positive pregnancy test.

> !!!!!! you left this behind,
> but we got to it first!
> meet you by the wall? R x

They know.
It's really real.
I've got to face it –

I've totally
screwed
up.

ZED
The four of us march around
the athletics track,
    far from listening ears.
You mustn't tell anyone,
    says Marnie fiercely,
taking the outside lane.

As if we would! Rakel exclaims.

She is jogging backwards,
   like this is a warm-up.
Maybe the test is wrong?

Marnie kicks a clod of earth
   & shakes her head.

She's quite correct.
I have already checked
   for a statistical margin of error
    & there is virtually none.
Pregnancy tests don't give false positives.

Rakel stops
   high-kneeing it
   backwards & forwards
   over the white-painted lines
& stretches out a hand to
   Marnie's stomach.
Well, hello, baby! she says.

Marnie jumps back like she's
   flinching from a punch.

MARNIE
Rakel reaches
to touch my tummy
like there's
already a little
human inside it,
a real, live,
kicking
baby.

Don't do that!

>   Rakel backs off, looking hurt.

>   Harry and his bunch of saddos
>   are kicking a ball
>   at the cricket nets.

>   *Hey, Marnie –*
>   Rakel lowers her voice
>   to a very loud whisper.
>   *The dad's not . . . ?*
>   She wrinkles her forehead.
>   *Please don't let it be . . . ?*
>   She screws up her nose.
>   *It isn't . . .*
>   she mouths,

>   *HARRY BORMAN?*

ZED
Harry Borman is exactly
    who I'm afraid it might be.

It hasn't escaped my attention how
    they avoid each other
    since the party.

Marnie throws back her head
    & laughs so hard,
    she coughs.

Oh, pur-lease! she says.
Give me credit for
    ***some** taste!*

I catch her eye &
>   for a long, looooooooong moment
>   we hold each other's gaze.

I remember her
>   standing at the top of Harry's stairs
>   straightening her skirt –
but that's Marnie's business,
>   not ours.

MARNIE
I hook Zed with a look
and he keeps his mouth shut.

Luca laughs and swats Rakel.
As if!

Then I'm saved by the hooter
for the end of lunch.

Laughing like that
nearly choked me,
but I think they swallowed it.

In English
the teacher says
we can sit where we like,
and like a shot
Rakel bags us a table for four.

We're supposed to be practising
long-form answers
but Rakel keeps pestering me
with short-form questions.

Who's the father?
So how did it happen?
How many weeks gone are you?
on a note passed under the table
to Zed – to Luca – to me.

She doesn't stop,
not even when I
scribble back,
Shut up!

ZED
All through geography
Rakel whispers, while
Marnie grows whiter,
    her lips tighter & tighter,
her fingers twisting
    a brand-new rubber into bits.

It's a constant stream of questions.
Rakel's tap is stuck at *on*.

On & on & on.

MARNIE
Rakel just won't shut up.
She hisses questions at me
like a leaking hose.

Does the father know? Do you love him? Have you told your mum? Are you still going to college? When's the baby due? Are you still going to college? Have you thought of any names? Will you breastfeed? Are you excited? Do you want a boy or a girl? What about stretch marks?

Have I thought of any names?
What the actual f—?!

I zone out and listen to
the teacher telling us
about watersheds,
a contour of high ground
from which the rainfall could
run off in

either direction.

Once it makes up its mind,
there's no going back.

I need to be by myself.
I need to think.

205

ZED
The second we're dismissed,
Marnie's off.

Rakel! For God's sake!
Why couldn't you give her some space?
Luca's shoving books in his bag
    fast as he can.
Run after her!
Say you're sorry!

Through the barrage of bodies
    making for the exit, I see
Rakel holding on to Marnie's blazer
    like the reins of a bolting horse.

                          MARNIE
                  Rakel won't let me go.

            Have you told the father?
              she's whisper-shouting,
                  hanging on to me
                    as I pull away.
            He might be really happy!
              Who is it? Who is it?
                      I won't tell!

            I've got to plug this,
                shut her up,
                    stop her
                    running on.

Have you thought that maybe
I'm not even sure
who the father is?
I snap.

She gasps, shocked.

I know I'm being mean,
but I can't stand her
happy-ever-after
attitude any more.

I shake her hand off.
I don't have to have it, you know!

Rakel's jaw drops
as she gets my meaning.
But, Marnie, you can't do that!

I stare at her in disbelief.
What does she mean,
I can't?

Doesn't she understand
that maybe I *must*?

ZED
Luca & I catch them up.
Rakel looks as if she's about to cry.
Marnie looks like a cornered tiger.
She says she might have a– have an– an–

Rakel is struggling to even say the word,
but we understand her meaning.

Luca puts a hand on Marnie's arm.
Please don't run off again! We'll help you.
We'll all support you, whatever you
   choose to do.

He glares at Rakel. *Isn't that right?*
But Rakel only bites her lip.

Luca turns to me, palms out.
Zed?

Me?
They're asking *me*?
Abortion isn't something
   I've thought about before.
It's a complex subject,
    & one to which I need to give
    a little thought.

It would be easy to say
   the wrong thing.

MARNIE
Zed just stands there stroking his chin
   without a word in my defence.

Rakel rubs at her mascara
and snivels, like it's
her disaster,
her decision,
her drama.

Luca's the only one on my side.
Marnie, he starts –

But I need to go
before I start to cry,
so I push past him,
half running, half walking,
and head for home
on foot.

I suppose I'll have to
tell my mum –
but how can I break the news
that I've let her down
in the worst way
I possibly
could?

As I walk, I put my hand on my belly,
which feels just like
my belly always does.
Nothing different.
Nothing special.

How can my body
possibly be
making a baby?

And I don't even want to *think*
about how it would
come out.

Me.
Me and a baby.

For a moment,
I imagine myself
walking this busy pavement
pushing a pretty baby in a pram.

Would it really be so bad?

Right on cue, a cross-faced woman
drags a screaming toddler
out from a shop.

Yes, it would.

ZED
In the awkward silence left by
   Marnie's angry exit,
   Rakel tries to explain herself.

It's not my fault, she says.
It's my faith. It's what I believe.
Sex is for making babies,
& babies are a gift from God.
*I can't **choose** not to think that way.*
It's part of me. My faith is in my bones.

Rakel reckons what you take into yourself as you grow –
   whether that's porridge or stories or God –
becomes part of you. Your DNA.

Marnie's got to give her baby
   a chance to live! she says,
      sliding her small silver crucifix
         along its chain.
            ✝

If you're not raised religious,
says Luca, *it's hard to get*
   where you're coming from, Rakel.
Personally,
I don't think it's
   any of my business
   what Marnie chooses to do
   with her own body, her own life –
so why is it any of yours?

Because abortion is just . . . ***wrong!***
Rakel stops short of saying murder,
but I think that's what she means.

I'm looking from one to the other,
   surprised at such strong views,
   amazed at such a chasm
   opening up between friends.

Beliefs are not something
   my mother & I
   have ever felt the need to discuss.

MARNIE
I'm calmer when I reach home.
Mum's in front of the telly but
   not watching it;
staring at her mobile instead.

The agency's
put me back on days,
she says, frowning.

When the car needs fixing,
when I'm busting out of uniform,
when we're down to the food bank again,
working nights brings in a bit more of the
(thinly sliced) bacon.

She puts her phone down with a sigh.
*This month we'll be lucky to
cover the car-park cost.*
Hospital staff don't even get
mate's rates.

All the things my mother could have done,
if it wasn't for me.

My phone bursts into life
before the tea is brewed.
Rakel's face lights up the screen.
I take it upstairs.

I'm hoping for an apology –
but is it, hell.

Have you considered adoption? she asks.

ADOPTION? Is she out of her tiny mind?
No, Rakel, I am not considering adoption.

Why not?

She's actually *serious*.

I take a deep breath and
let her have it.

So why on earth wouldn't I want to lug a baby around for months, get stretch-marked and sick, with everyone asking me all the time who the father is – and no, Rakel, it's none of your business – and I'd almost certainly lose my place at college, wouldn't go to art school and I'd be branded a slut forever; I'd lose any trust that I have restored with my mum (who, by the way, was faced with the same dilemma and chose to keep me even though I messed up her life) – and, oh my God, what if my mother wanted to adopt my baby, could you imagine it, a brother or sister who is actually my own child, that is horrific – and what if I loved it and couldn't give it up, and what if I didn't love it and then I was just a monster? So yes, I've considered adoption and you can take your advice and shove it right up –

but Rakel's hung up.

After Mum leaves for work that night

I sit cross-legged on my bed,
staring out of the window
while the sun goes down.

Gradually, the light
fades from the sky
until it's
as dark as
Harry's room.

Don't worry, babe,
his voice said in the black,
I got this covered.

I want to
turn back time.

Chapter Twenty

ZED
When I should be
    sitting at my desk revising physics
    I'm disappearing down
        a Reddit
          rabbit
            hole.

I learn that
    abortion is so divisive,
  so wrapped up in faith & morality,
  it splits countries down the middle.

In America, state after state
    is turning off the lights
    on women's rights.

There are protests & counterprotests
    all over the world.

Even in this country, abortion
    is tantamount to taboo.
No one likes to talk about it.

Everybody shouts
    about having sex all the time,
but abortion, it would appear,
is secret & shameful.

No wonder Marnie wants
    to keep this quiet.

Three hours into my research, my eyeballs have been roasted by the online flame wars. People's gods clashing with laws clashing with women's rights clashing with men's opinions clashing with medicine clashing with ethics. The arguments about when life begins rampage back & forth across my polarised screen until I stare at clumps of pixels which represent cells which represent potential humans & I'm sure of only one thing. Whatever conclusion I do – or don't – come to, doesn't really matter.

All that matters –
    all that *should* matter –
        is what Marnie thinks.

It's *her* body.
Her life.
Her choice.

MARNIE
For the third time, my phone shatters the night.
    It's Zed again.
    I give in and pick up.

If you're here to have a go at me
for pissing off Rakel,
I'm not in the mood!
I'm not in the mood for anything.

There's half a beat
    before Zed says,
    I'm sorry.

The word sounds stiff,
    as if it's foreign.

I give him no words of my own.
I want him to feel
how much not speaking hurts.

The silence stretches
between ——————— us
like a wire
until finally
Zed clears his throat.

If a specific apology is required,
then I apologise.
I'm sorry I didn't stand up for you.
I should have told Rakel that
it wasn't her decision to make.
*It has to be **your** choice.*
How can I help?

Now it's
my turn
not to speak.

ZED
I never heard anyone
    cry so hard before.

It sounds incredibly messy,
& I'm very uncomfortable.

After an eternity or two,
    Marnie hiccups to a halt.

I know I've got the right
   to choose for myself . . .
She sniffs.
But how do I make that decision?
Everything I can do right now
feels wrong.

I drag a line through
~~tonight's revision plans~~
& open up Excel.

MARNIE
Zed shares a spreadsheet with me
and I fill it in.

ARGUMENTS FOR HAVING THE BABY	ARGUMENTS FOR *NOT* HAVING THE BABY
Mum kept me	I don't want to be as broke as Mum
Mum will help me	Mum never has to know
Babies are quite cute	I know nothing about babies
I could go to art college later	I want to go to art college NOW
Will an abortion hurt?	Birth *definitely* hurts
Rakel will judge me	Everyone will judge me
How could I kill a baby?	How could I mess up my own life?
It's Harry's baby too	I don't want Harry involved
I'll have someone to love me	Who would marry me with a baby?
I might be a great mum	I'll probably be a terrible mum
Not facing pro-life protesters	Facing teachers at school

ZED
Next, I ask her to *weight* her issues,
give each a number from one to ten,
rank them in order of importance.

Pro-CHOICE outweighs Anti-ABORTION by far,
but still Marnie hesitates.
I – I don't know . . . she says.
She sounds panicked.
She's full of guilt.

Time to intervene.
*Why don't we decide **your** way?* I say.
Let's toss a coin.

WHAT? She's shocked.

I put the phone down for a moment.
Got one! I call from the other side of the room.
Heads for not having the baby, okay?
I promise I won't cheat.
Flipping it now . . . & . . . & . . . oh – hang on,
I've dropped it.
Got it.
It's . . . . tails.

I come back to the phone.
That's decided then.
*You're **having** the baby.*

This should settle it. I wait for
Marnie's reaction.

MARNIE
SERIOUSLY? You're nuts.
You can't decide something like this
on a throw of the dice!

ZED
Actually, it was a toss of a coin.

MARNIE
Whatever.
I'm not having a baby
because your bloody coin says so!
Are you freakin' insane, playing games with –

ZED
Marnie shouts.
I hold the phone away from my ear.
Marnie doesn't realise that
    tossing a coin
is the psychological version of a litmus test:
it reveals what you're feeling, deep inside.

When the danger of being deafened has passed,
I inform her that, even if she didn't know it,
    she has already decided
    she doesn't want this baby.
If she did, she'd have welcomed the result.

It's not actually about the coin throw, Marnie.

MARNIE
Oh.
The penny drops.
There never was a coin, was there?

ZED
No.
Just like there never was a cat.

MARNIE
So now I know what I want,
how do I get it?

Of course Zed's already researched
the heck out of it. He sends me a link.
You don't have to go to a clinic, he says.
You fill this in & they call you back.

ZED
The questions on the clinic form are very intrusive.

Marnie snorts. *You think **this** is intrusive?*
You should try having sex.

No, thanks.

Marnie says she knows
all the dates they need.

I think I also know one of those dates,
but we don't
discuss it.

MARNIE
I'm glad that Zed can't see my screen,
the stuff they ask.
But finally the form is finished.

This is my watershed moment.
I breathe deep and press submit.

That's it.
No going back.

Chapter Twenty-One

ZED
After last night's long call with Marnie
I felt very unstable: I could neither
    study nor sleep.
As a consequence, this morning
    my brain is much
    blurrier than I'd like.

MARNIE
After last night's call with Zed
I feel so much clearer.
Calmer. I know where I'm heading.

ZED
I'm going to Oxford University today
for the last lap of the Marathon.

If I'm going to tread in the footsteps
    of my physics heroes,
I really need to
    put my best foot
        forward.

It's the last day of the Easter term –
also the last day of normality
    for Year 11s.
Predictably, the bus to school is bubbling,
full of students fizzing
    like a shaken bottle of Coke.

I clamp my headphones on my head
    like a hard hat,
for protection.

MARNIE
In physics, Ms Rahman
asks for a volunteer
to hand out
revision packs.

Jessica Bates' hand shoots up.
Please, miss, let me! she says,
uncharacteristically
eager to help.

What's she up to?

Jessica hurls the handouts round
but lingers when she gets to my desk.
With a French-tipped fingernail
she taps the sheaf of paper and whispers,
***Someone* left *something* lying on the floor!**
She tut-tuts and moves on.

I pick the pack up.
There's a loose sheet lying underneath
which isn't physics.

I look closer
and the world stops.

It's a photocopy of the note Rakel and I
passed in class.
Our handwriting is eclipsed
by a big, black-Sharpied threat.

I feel myself
go faint
with fear.

ZED
Mother will give me a lift to the Marathon.
She'll pick me up after period one.

I'm just having a precautionary pee
    when I hear raised voices from the girls' side.
I hesitate with
    one hand on my fly.

> ***TELL ME
> WHO THE FATHER IS,
> YOU SLAG!***

Jessica Bates' voice vaults
the white-tiled wall.

I zip up, quick.

Marnie's in trouble.

MARNIE
Jessica's got me
bent backwards by the basins,
her furious face stuck in mine,
her fingers pinching
a twist of my skin to fire.

If it was Harry . . . she hisses,
*if you tell **anyone** Harry is the father* –
Jessica holds her phone level
with my eyeballs –
I'm sending this!

> MARNIE STAEDLERS
> PREGNANT!
> DIRTY BITCH

A text written ready to
ruin my life – as if my life
wasn't ruined already.

The smell of Jessica's cherry vape
messes with the stink of toilet cleaner
and my gut *rolls over.*

Her fingertip still hovers over *send.*

If I tell Jessica the truth, I think she might stab me.
I bet she's tooled up.
A sharpened nail file
would be just
her style.

How can I convince her it wasn't Harry?

Five!

She's counting. How can I stop that text?

Four!

I'll just give her a name –

Three!

Any name.
Anything to throw her off the scent.
I spit a hank of white-blonde hair
from my mouth, suck in air –

Two!

There's a cough! from the doorway.
It's Zed.

Zed! I shout.

Zed's *the father?* Jessica snarls.
Don't lie to me, Marnie!
I'm gonna tell the world
that you're a ho.

ZED
Me?

                MARNIE
       Zed's eyes are like ping-pong balls
         spinning in the lottery draw.

                Please, Zed!
            I beg him silently.
     We'll sort it out later, I promise.

ZED
Me?
This is outrageous!

But yesterday I let Marnie down.
I kept quiet when I should have spoken up.
Perhaps I can protect her now.

I clear my throat. *It's true.*
Whatever Marnie has told you
   is the truth.
I am, indeed, the father.

                MARNIE
           Jessica's shiny lips
    stretch out in a Bond-villain smile.
      Oh . . . my . . . days! she says.

       Zed, you had us all fooled!

Sorry, Marnie, but . . .
Her talon tap-taps at the screen.
Zed's been a naughty boy?
This is too good not to share.

ZED
When she
hits *send*,
there's
a sound
which reflects exactly
   how Jessica Bates
    is now flushing
     my life down
     the lavatory.

        whooooooosh!   it goes.

The second it's sent
I wish I could retract,
    rescind,
        hit CTL+Z on what I said.

Arriving just too late to save me,
my phone blares the *Ride of the Valkyries*,
announcing my mother's impatience.

I run.

What have I done?

MARNIE
What have I done?

What have I done, what have I done, what have I done?
What have I done, what have I done, what have I done?
What have I done, what have I done, what have I done?
What have I done, what have I done, what have I done?

At the bottom of the art-room cupboard I curl
into the tightest of balls,
taking the smallest
space I can.

I can't get any lower.
I am pond life.

Against my cheek
my phone vibrates,
outraged.

Chapter Twenty-Two

ZED
What have I done?

I slump in Mother's car, knowing I'll be
    social mincemeat
        in minutes.

As we reach Oxford, it's apparent that my mother –
usually such a meticulous organiser –
hasn't planned our parking.

She drives fruitlessly
    through the ancient streets
    until we find a spot. We are late,
the last to collect our name tags.

Officials look at our tardiness askance,
& seal my phone into a plastic bag
    as though they know
    it's toxic.

What have I done?

We walk into an echoing chamber.
The pillars of stone & vaulted ceiling
    are straight out of Hogwarts.
We're sorted:
parents to the left   children to the right.

One hundred of the UK's
    top-performing physics students
    are gathered, patches of
    coloured blazers clumping together.
I am the only one in Downham's dark blue.

The other parents leave the hall with hugs,
    my mother with a tense smile.

What have I done?

We're herded to tiny wooden desks.
I cast covert glances at my rivals.
They look more relaxed than me:
no sweat rings under armpits,
    no tics, stims, chewed lips or tears.

I try to limber up
    with some comforting laps of Collatz conjecture
but even this simple sequence of numbers
    is beyond me today.

All I can think about
    is the online amphitheatre in which
    my private life is being paraded,
    my dignity destroyed.

From the portrait gallery of Oxford greats,
Tim Berners-Lee stares down
    dispassionately.

What have I done?

The dean's voice booms like a starting gun.
Welcome, students, to the final of the prestigious
    British Schools Physics Marathon!

The test to decide my future
    has begun.

MARNIE

The cupboard door swings slowly open.

Marnie?

It's Naomi.
I thought I saw you dash in there! she says.
What are you looking f—?
Her voices changes. *Oh, hey . . .*
Who're you hiding from?

Everyone.
I'm hiding from everyone.
But most of all
from myself.

I don't feel well,
I say,
and it's true.
I am sick at myself.

ZED
An hour later,
three quarters of the time is gone,
& I've only attempted half the questions.

Around me, a few have finished.
I'm being lapped.
I want to focus on the lovely logic,
the peaceful progression of numbers,
but there are sweat-smears on my paper &
    the formulae are swimming –
I have to blink them clear.

Pens down!

Outside, Mother asks how I did,
    but I just shake my head.

While the papers are marked,
we tour the physics labs &
    learn about the advancements made
    by famous Oxford names.

The World Wide Web, wave functions, gravitational singularity, Hawking radiation, black holes & time travel, the Hubble Space Telescope, proof of the expanding universe . . .

I watch the glittering prizes slide out of my reach.

No summer-school fast track
    to the selective scientific sixth form,
        so maybe
            no Oxford
                after all.

I am too disappointed to speak.

We are called, one by one,
    to shake the beaming warden's hand.
I'm damp-palmed, my fingers limp
    with let-down.
We pose for photographs, but
    I cannot say *cheese* for the camera.

Mother hasn't cracked a smile
    all day.

What have I done?

Chapter
Twenty-Three

ZED
I just want to go home.

Mother & I do not linger over the goodbyes.
Back in the car
    I fasten my seat belt,
        clamp on my headphones
        & turn on my phone.

Within seconds
my face is on fire.
It's actually *worse*
    than I could have imagined.
In less than the time it's taken
    to tank a test,
    my private life has been
    d-i-s-s-e-c-t-e-d,

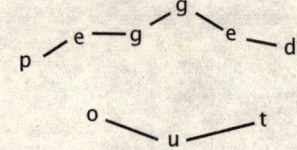

on the slab of social media.

The comments are scrolling
    almost too fast to read –
opinions, speculation,
    about me, about Marnie.

I will never forgive myself for this mistake.
I slide the screen to black.

At home, I go straight to my room.

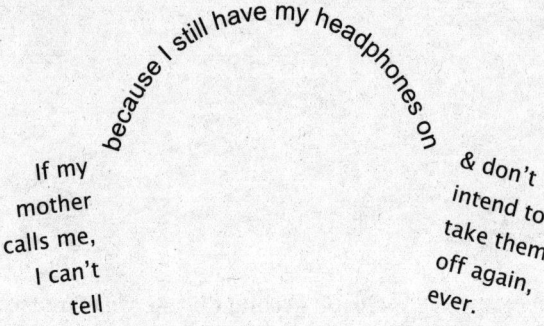

because I still have my headphones on

If my mother calls me, I can't tell

& don't intend to take them off again, ever.

Rain falls through the greyish
   mid-afternoon light.
I draw my blinds to
   seal myself inside.

I don't plan to emerge
   until next term.

I'm putting my life
   (what's left of it)
   on airplane mode.

MARNIE
The bus is late and it's raining.
Of course it is.
Great fat pelting raindrops, hard as hailstones.
I read the messages about me and Zed,
tucking my phone under my coat
to keep it dry.

So many, I can't keep up.

One blink, and the counter changes from

287

to

291

insults piling on top of each other
like a rugby scrum.

In our private group,
Rakel and Luca
are trying to
talk to me.

Jessica's spreading such shit
about you two! hv u seen it?

she's told everyone
marnie's pregnant!

she says zed's the dad??????!

wanna damp it down, but . . .
☹

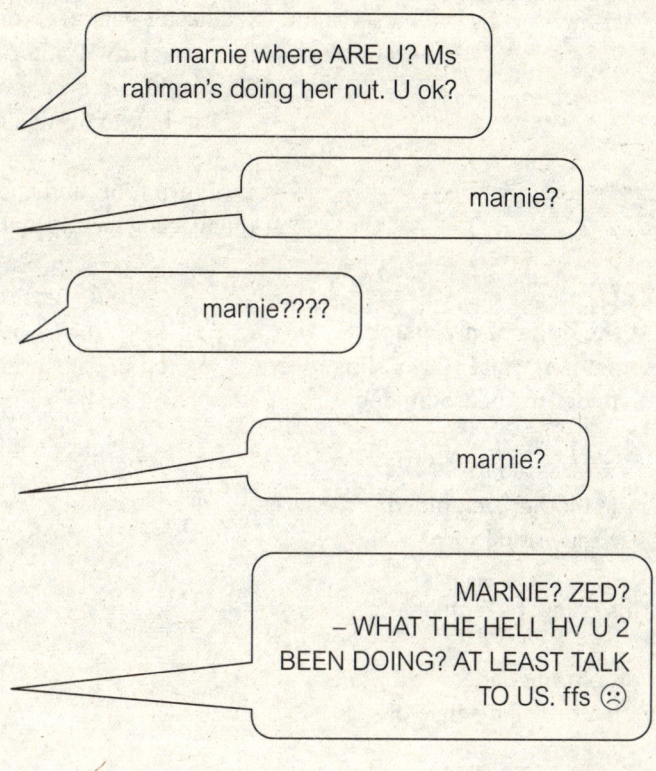

They're so angry
I leave the group.

I'm dripping as I
trudge up our stinking stairwell
and turn my key in the gritty lock.

Mum's still at work, thank God.
I slump into the armchair
and for the zillionth time,
check my phone.

Zed hasn't messaged me.
Why would he?
Why would Zed ever want
to talk to me again?

I turn it off and stare
at the black screen instead.

ZED
At the edge of my vision,
something white slowly slips
under my bedroom door.

It's addressed to *Zebedee*
in Mother's cramped
handwriting.

This is most irregular.

I unfold the paper
with a growing sense of
dread.

MARNIE
I don't know how long it is
before the living-room light clicks on
and Mum stands in the doorway,
rain dripping off her mac.

Marnie?
What's going on?
You haven't even started on tea!

She's angry.

I try to answer,
but all that comes out is a croak.

Next thing,
Mum is kneeling by my side,
her wet arm chill around my shoulders.
My head is buried against her chest.

I could be three again,
a toddler with a bloodied knee.

*Love? What's wrong?
What's the matter?*

My tears arrive in a torrent,
too fast for talking.

ZED

*Zebedee, I would like to talk to you,
but you are not picking up your
phone or your messages, and there
was no response to my knock.
Please could you come to my study?
It's urgent.*

Mother

MARNIE
***I'm sorry I shouted,* says Mum.**
She's rubbing my back.
It's been a tough day.
Take a deep breath –
that'll help.

There are no breaths
deep enough for this.

How can I break
the news that will
smash her heart
to pieces?

Mum pulls out her tissues.
Here, blow.
She throws the empty pack away.
I've mopped up a lot of tears today, she says,
at the Bealing Centre.

The Bealing? I sit up.
That's the sexual-health clinic
where you can get condoms –
or if it's too late for prevention,
at least some help to sort out your mess.

Mum's working there?
Oh no.

She gives my shoulders a squeeze.
*At least that's **one** bit of trouble*
you haven't bought home!
You know better, right?
After the mistake your mother made.
She feels me pull away
and adds quickly –
Not that I don't love my mistake, of course!

Mum tips a finger to lift my chin.
Anyway . . . what's up?
Whatever it is, you can tell me.

But I can't. Not now.
I can't even look her
in the eye.

ZED
I search Mother's face for clues & notice
    the creases on her forehead are
    slightly sharper, as though they've
    come into focus.

She switches off her monitor &
    gestures for me to sit.

Is she ill? Is it cancer?
A beat begins in the angle of my jaw.

Perhaps I should have told you before –
she coughs uncomfortably –
    but I was hoping
    the situation would resolve itself.

I wait for her to say more, but
    at least a *situation*
    doesn't sound like
    cancer.

The truth is, she says,
    addressing the door frame,
    I might have lost my job.

Well.
I was not expecting that.

MARNIE
I'm expecting.
Isn't that what people say?
I'm in the family way.
I'm going to have a baby.

But I don't want to tell my mum
    any of those things.
    I don't want to tell her
    I'm pregnant
    at all.

I push myself out of her arms.
    Nothing!
    It's nothing.
    Forget it.

I have to sort this out for myself.
Isn't that what Mum always wants,
    for me to take responsibility?

> I can hear her voice saying,
> *You made this mess, Marnie.
> Now get yourself out of it.*
>
> Well, I will.
>
> I should have an email from the clinic by now.
> I go up to my room and wait
> for my creaking laptop
> to fire up.

ZED
My mother is afraid of being fired.

Why?
She made a most uncharacteristic mistake.
A hairline crack of code,
    the tiny line of difference
    between a minus & a plus.

But it was repeated & reflected
    & multiplied in a mirror maze
    over & over & over
    until the error was

enormous.

I should have told someone, she's saying,
*but I didn't want to blemish my record by
    admitting to such a careless error.*

All those late nights working?
Mother was trying to
    patch the holes,
    untangle the knots,
    paper over the cracks.

But the holes got deeper,
    the knots more gnarled,
& the cracks grew so wide
    they were chasms.

A simple *we-can-fix-this-if-we-work-together*
    mishap
became a monumental
    this-could-cost-millions-in-reputational-damage
    full-blown crisis.

This morning she finally
    asked for help.

She says
    now it's out there,
    now the worst has happened,
she feels almost
    relieved.

MARNIE
I could cry with relief.
The appointment's come through.
The clinic will call me on Monday
at 9:45 a.m.

I turn my phone back on
but Rakel keeps calling,
so I block her.

I don't care that Rakel would do
what my mother did
and have the baby.
This is happening to *me*.

It's *my* body.
My life.
My choice.

ZED
The company has no choice,
Mother says,
her thin finger tracing a groove in the armrest,
but to 'consider my position'.

Which means they might sack her.

In which case, she says,
*sixth-form school fees
will no longer be a
financial possibility.*

Mother has been excluded from work
until a decision is made.
She is expecting an email next week.

Chapter
Twenty-Four

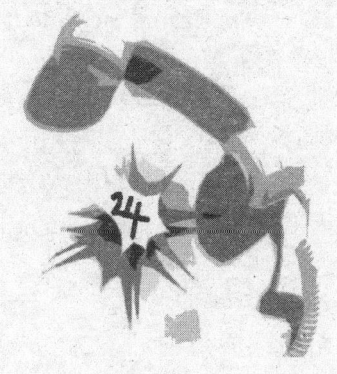

MARNIE

At
9:30
my alarm goes off.

I switch my phone from airplane mode
and watch it
like a cat at a mousehole
while I brush my teeth.

Cleaning my teeth makes me gag –
everything makes me feel sick these days.

I'm rinsing the taste from my mouth
when a

ring! ring! ring!

sends my heart into spasm.

It's the clinic!

I grab my mobile with hands that are
suddenly slippery with sweat.

Hello?

ZED
I can't believe
    Mother hid this from me.

Weeks of her worrying &
    weeks of me studying,
      for a school we can
    no longer afford.

What a waste.

Why didn't she say something?

MARNIE
It's not the clinic. It's Rakel.

Marnie? Finally!

          She must've hidden behind 141.

You wouldn't answer my calls. Let's talk –

          I hit the red button.
          I don't want to talk to her,
          not until it's over.

          She has her opinion. I have mine.
          It's *my* choice –
          however hard.

ZED
Mother agrees we need to talk, even if it's hard.
We go for a walk, side by side
    so we don't have to look into
    each other's faces.

MARNIE
No Caller ID
flashes up again immediately.

Piss off, Rakel!
I go to my settings
and ~~block~~ unknown callers.

9:47

Why hasn't the clinic rung?

9:48

I'm such an idiot!
I unblock and instantly –

ring!
ring!
ring!

ZED
We walk rings around the park pond,
    my mother & I,
        opening conversational windows,
    letting the air in, sharing.

Emotions are a foreign language,
    hard to speak, difficult to understand.

We get overheated drinks
    from the cafe by the entrance
    & sit on a bench decorated by ducks.

I tell her how different I am from my peers –
    which seems to come as
    no surprise to her.

She tells me how afraid of failure
    she has become.
I understand.

I blow on my hot chocolate
    to encourage evaporative cooling,
& tell her other people's expectations feel
    as restrictive & as artificial
    as an iron lung.
They pressurise me into a passion I don't feel.
They ask me *who* I want to be with,
    not *if* I want to be with
    anyone at all.

My mother sips her coffee & listens quietly.
When I tell her what was written
    on the graffiti wall, she raises an eyebrow.
You should have told me, she says.

We agree we have allowed
    the gap between us
    to grow too wide.

I'm sorry, we say,
    the underused word
    creaking on our scalded tongues.

I'm sorry.
I tell her I have fallen out with Marnie –
    but I don't say why.
That isn't
    my secret to share.

MARNIE
The nurse from the clinic
shares her name. *Sherana.*
Her voice is smooth and sweet like chocolate.

She says I'm sensible to seek help.
Her words are gentle with my feelings,
as if she thinks I deserve kindness.
She doesn't tell me how
    stupid I am –
but says I should come to the clinic
    and have a dating scan.

Go into the clinic
and risk bumping into Mum,
take the chance of coming face to face
with placard-waving protesters?

No way.

I tell her I'm sure of my dates.
I got my period on my
second day at Downham High,
and I will never ever, *ever* forget
the night of the party.

I've counted the sixteen squares
between those two dates so often,
I've worn a path
through the pages
of my planner.

I reassure her that
my periods were regular,
my fanny doesn't smell funny,
I'm not bleeding and nothing hurts
(except my breasts).
That's all good, she says. *In that case
we don't need to see you.*

But my relief
doesn't last long.
Sherana clears her throat.
Sorry, she says gently,
*but I have to ask this.
Do you know who the father is?*

The answer
makes me choke
on the injustice of it all.
*Of course I do!
I've only had sex once,
and he didn't even finish!*

Sherana agrees I was most unlucky.
She agrees it isn't fair.

She wishes people didn't think
it can't happen the first time,
she wishes we didn't think
pulling out will work –

I didn't think that!
I protest –

but she calmly carries on.

She asks if he's much older than me.
It's about safeguarding,
she says.

He's in my year, I say bitterly.
*He's barely over sixteen –
just like his IQ.*

Sherana doesn't laugh.
She asks if I consented.

I snort.
*To getting pregnant? No.
But if you mean the sex part,
I guess I did.
At least he stopped
when I changed my mind.*

Okay, she says. *That's okay then.*

I don't agree that it's okay,
but he hasn't broken any laws
as far as I know.

Now, as you're eight weeks and five days gone –

I almost choke.
WHAT? Eight weeks?
But I gave you the date –
the party was only six weeks ago!

Honey, we date your pregnancy
from the first day of your last period,
Sherana explains, like she's said this
many times before.
Don't worry – lots of girls get that wrong.

Stupid! Stupid! Stupid me!
I want to punch my temples.
Does that mean I'm too late?

No, it's okay,
says Sherana.
You've still got time.
You're fine.

I'm still under the

10 week

limit
for pills by post,
for dealing with it at home.

But there's still another
humiliating hoop
to jump through.
Sherana says if Harry gave me a baby,
maybe he gave me an infection as well.
She says she'll include an STI test to check.

Sexually transmitted infections
can be very harmful
if left untreated,
she says.

If Harry's given me an infection,
I'll bloody kill him.
How's *that* for harmful?
But to Sherana,
I just say,
Gotcha.

Now . . .
Sherana pauses.
This is really important.
You should have an adult with you
when you go through this.
Will someone be at home?

Um . . . yeah . . . my mum.
I could do it
when she's off-shift,
hide away in my room
and she'll never know.

So, is she there now, love?
We'll need a chat, check she can support you.

NO! I say quickly.
I mean - sorry, no.
I mean, I - I can't tell her.
Is that a problem?

I'm not allowed to do this at home
if I'm on my own.

If there's no other adult I trust, she says
it could be a friend my age.

*But I need to talk to them,
to make sure they're competent,
they're confident,
they can cope.*

She says she'll check in with me tomorrow,
but what's the point?
I'm stuffed.

The only friends I have who fit the bill
both hate me.

The doorbell rings as we end the call.
I run downstairs,
hoping it's Zed or Luca,
that I'm saved,
but instead,
blocking the doorstep,
is a box with human legs.

What the . . . ?

A familiar Afro
pokes over the top
and a voice says,
Hi! Are you feeling better now?

It's Naomi. Naomi? What's she doing here?

Naomi thrusts the box towards me.
*You went home before
I could teach you how to use*

*the silk screen frame. Maybe
you can make some paper-cut prints
over the holidays, for your portfolio?*

She puts a finger to her lips.
*Shhh!
It's a bit . . . um, unofficial . . .
I got your address from Luca.
But I think you'll be great at printing.*

Her confidence in me hurts.
She has no idea
what a mess-up I am.
Sorry, Naomi, I don't think I can –

Just take it!
The box is surprisingly light,
with a familiar chemical smell.

Naomi grins. *You'll be fine.
There are loads of videos online
for paper-cut printing;
it's simple enough at home.*

Then she backs away
before I can give the box back.

It's all about control and care, she says.
*Watch it with the craft knife, and
don't drag that squeegee
too quick or too slow.*

She turns to go.
*Don't forget to record
everything you do
in your portfolio!*

I watch her drive away in a flower-painted mini,
then lug the massive box up to my tiny room.

In bed again, I pull up the covers.
Why not distract myself
with screen-printing videos?
At least it's more productive
than panicking.

ZED
At the end of our walk,
Mother & I agree
this has been a most
productive exchange.

From now on, every Sunday at 3 p.m.
our smart speaker will remind us
to have a mother & son check-in.

MARNIE
Two hours later, I'm still learning
about screen printing.
Wow.

Cutting the paper masks is simple,
like Naomi said, but it's only the start,
the very beginning of printing.

I could do so much more
with access to the acetates
at school.

Videos show me
the way to
split the colours,
print the templates,
block out the light to let
the chemical alchemy of emulsion
work its magic on the screen.

So many techniques!
duotone, halftone, spot colour, greyscale,
linocut, block print, letter print, mono.

So many applications!
I could work on ad campaigns and illustrations.
I could get a job in graphics, repro or even publishing.

If I get my diploma –
if I make it to art school –
I can learn a skill to earn my living.

Naomi did me a bigger favour than she knew.
There are entire *minutes* this morning
when I don't think about
being pregnant –
at least
until
the tender image of
a duotone Madonna cradling her baby
brings me back down to
earth with a

bump.

Chapter Twenty-Five

25 ← (Actually not 25 cos i ran out of room)
REASONS TO FORGIVE ME ...

MARNIE
For my first attempt,
I trace the letter shapes on newsprint paper
and cut them out with care,
stick the paper to the screen,
drag the squeegee through the ink
(not too fast, not too slow)
first one way then back again –
and make
my first
ever
screen print.

I hold it to the light.
It's crap.
The register's all wrong
and the words are patchy,
like I don't really mean them.

I try again and again
because my message
really matters.

ZED
I've completed five of Easter's fourteen days
& one hundred per cent of the homework.

Life is as quiet as it used to be
    before I met Marnie.

Considering it is switched off,
I'm not surprised at the silence from my phone,
but there's been
    no news at all from my mother's office.

We're starting to twitch with the tension.

MARNIE
At teatime
Mum and I sit
across a chasm of silence.

Mum throws the occasional conversational rope, like
How did the designing go? and *Can I help with revision?*
but her chat falls short, slipping uselessly
off my single syllables.

I'm too nervous, too guilty, to respond.
Every minute that passes
my unspoken lie grows bigger,
my little bundle of cells
becomes more real.
I have to get this done.
Now.

I get up from the table.
I'm going out.

Outside, the air is thick and soft,
full of secrets.
I catch the bus to Zed's.

ZED
I'm having a go at Spanish.
I've had to resort to an app.
I'm parroting back words
    I don't understand
when I hear the flap of the letterbox spring back.

A moment later, Mother taps on the door,
    an outsized postcard in her hand.

For you, I assume?

I take it & look closer:
it's off-centre,
the edges of the letters have bled
& it's a little messed up.
Must be from Marnie.

On the back of the postcard, she has sketched
a rather inaccurate representation of
    an Excel spreadsheet.

On the left, the reasons why I should forgive her.
On the right, more reasons.

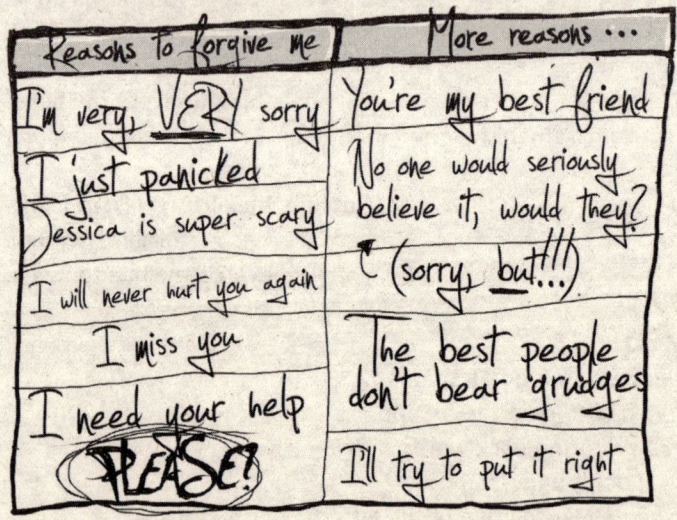

Marnie is flipping a two-headed coin.

Laughing
 makes me realise
 how much I have missed her.

MARNIE
Zed texts me
while I'm still on my way to Luca's.

> Forgiveness duly granted.
> What else do you need?

Here goes.

ZED
If I don't stay with her when she takes the pills,
Marnie says she'll have to go into the clinic.

The clinic where her mum might be.

MARNIE
I'm not ready to tell Mum. Not yet.
She's going to be so upset.
& what if she wants me
to have the baby, like she did?
It's her flesh and blood, after all.

ZED
Marnie's afraid of facing protesters.

> **MARNIE**
> **There's a protection zone,**
> like a circle they can't go inside –
> but my mum told me
> the picketers
> camp around the edge.
>
> Without a car, you'd have to
> tunnel your way in
> to avoid them.
>
> I've seen it on TV,
> the angry crowds yelling, the tears,
> the upsetting images waved
> in women's faces.

ZED	**MARNIE**
She doesn't need	**I don't need**
that hating,	that hating,
not when	not when
she hates herself	I hate myself
so much	so much
already.	already.

Poor Marnie.

But to give a definite answer,
I need to know what to expect,
what will happen
    exactly.

Googling reveals that
abortion is definitely not for wimps.
But then, neither is childbirth.

The more I learn about female biology,
the more grateful I am
    to have a penis.

MARNIE
Zed said *yes!*
Not only that, but
he sends across
a list of links
on the
pills-by-post
medical abortion process.

Screen-printing	*Abortion.*
Terribly	Terribly
complicated	simple
for something so	for something so
simple.	complicated.

Once again I crawl under my duvet
and wade through info on the web.
Not nearly as nice as screen-printing,
but really quite straightforward.

Sherana calls.
I pass on Zed's number.

ZED
A nurse called Sherana
    speaks to me as though I'm an idiot
    unversed in human biology.

I recite back the circumstances
    under which we should seek help.

The parameters are helpfully precise
    & easy to understand –

an enormous improvement on Spanish.

                                                MARNIE
                                      Sherana's satisfied
                                          that Zed can cope.

                                  She agrees to send me
                                        the pills by
                                    next-day delivery.

                                          I'm so nearly
                                          not pregnant.

Chapter Twenty-Six

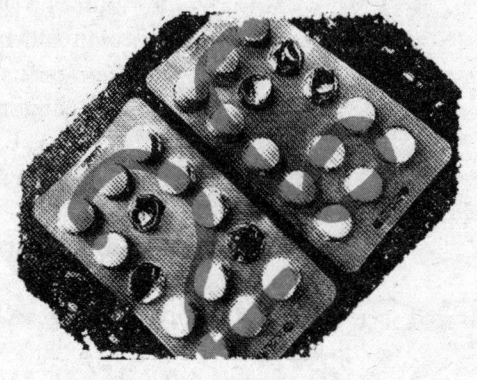

MARNIE
The next morning
an innocently plain
brown cardboard package
plops on the mat.

I race down the stairs
to grab it before Mum does.

Inside is an abortion bento box:
lots of little packets of pills,
a pregnancy test to use three weeks later,
the swab for STIs (*urgh*)
and a handful of colourful condoms.

A bit late for the condoms now,
but I appreciate
the thought.

This time, I read the instructions.
Then I read them again.
And a third time, just to be sure.

I have to take one pill to
halt the pregnancy and
four different pills
the next day.

There
are two
extra pills
in case I need
a bit of a boost.

Also the promised
bubble strip of painkillers.

When I asked Sherana
if it would hurt,
she was quite clear –
Yes. It will.

Everybody's different, she said,
*but imagine a really, really bad period.
At least it's over quite quickly.*

I'm glad it's going to hurt.
I *need* it to hurt.
I need to pay penance.

My bedroom is hushed and still,
the windows shut, the curtains drawn
against the morning traffic.
It feels as solemn as church.

Before I start, I go online again.
At eight weeks,
what is inside me
is no longer a speck of a seed –
it's the size and shape
of a butter bean.

I know I'm torturing myself,
but I need to understand
what I'm doing.
Face up to it.

Be brave.

I hold my hand
to the flat plane of belly
where my own
butter bean
is hiding.

Poor little embryo, I whisper to it.
*Poor thing, trying to grow
in me.*

At exactly midday
I pop the first pill from its packet.
My fingers are trembling.

Be brave.

Sorry, I whisper to my little legume.
Sorry, sorry, sorry.

I take a sip of water
and
swallow.

That afternoon I stay in my room.
I'm supposed to be revising,
but I can't concentrate,
nothing sticks in my head
though at least the pill stays down.

It's nearly over,
I tell myself.

Hang on.

The next morning
I tell Mum I need Zed's help.
She assumes I mean with physics.

ZED
Sherana said Marnie should be at home
& not alone,
but she didn't say *whose* home,
so Marnie is coming to mine.

MARNIE
We tell Zed's dragon mother we're revising
but she scarcely puffs smoke
from her study.

Up in Zed's bedroom
I lay out the contents of
the bento box, while
Zed googles the chemicals.

ZED
I think we have
all the equipment we need.

- 4 x Misoprostol tablets to make Marnie's womb contract (plus 2 extra in case)
- Codeine
- Sanitary towels the size of small pillows
- Spanish & physics textbooks
- Chocolate milkshake
- Tortilla chips
- Two supermarket slabs of chocolate
- A family bag of jelly babies

On further reflection,
when Marnie's in the bathroom,
I put the jelly babies back in my drawer.

> **MARNIE**
> **In Zed's posh ensuite bathroom**
> I push the pills up high inside me.
> It's embarrassing,
> and I could have just
> tucked them in my cheek,
> but Zed's research
> says it's better
> in case I'm sick.
>
> Zed's very reassuring.

ZED
I'm very nervous.
While we wait for the symptoms to start,
we do a mock Spanish oral,
meaning Marnie mocks my mistakes.

We accidentally finish the snacks.

> **MARNIE**
> **Two and half hours later,**
> there's a low ache in my belly
> which grows to a growl.

ZED
Marnie's mouth goes tight. She breathes in sharply.
She wants to watch a Disney movie
& I cannot reasonably object.

MARNIE
The cramps are coming in waves.
The pills are working.
I'm bleeding.
I'm losing my pregnancy.

Zed says if we watch the sequel,
by the end it could all be over.
But the movie was a mistake:
all that saccharine smugness
is making me feel sick.

Let it go, I tell Zed.
He switches it off with an
audible sigh of relief.

ZED
Marnie refuses the last bit of chocolate
with a swear word that's
more like a moan.

MARNIE
OHHHHHHHHH!
This hurts, this really hurts.

ZED
She grabs my hand & squeezes hard.
Now we're both uncomfortable.

MARNIE
I'm holding Zed's hand. I can't let go.
He offers me codeine and I say no.

                                                        I *want* to hurt.
                                            This is my penance.

                  I try not to think about what's happening.

                                   I hold Zed's hand as
                          the hurting comes in waves.
                          I want my back massaged.

                                        I want my mum.

ZED
Marnie won't let me call her mum,
so I phone the 24/7 aftercare number.
Does she have a temperature? the voice asks.

I touch her forehead, then mine. No fever.
Marnie goes to check her pad, to
    make sure the bleeding's not too heavy.
It's not, she calls. *But there are clots! Lots!*
She sounds shocked.

The voice says everything is normal. *Try to relax.*
Relax? They cannot be serious.
I massage some feeling back into my fingers.

Marnie needs more hands-on comfort
    than I feel comfortable with.
Call Luca! she groans.

With some relief,
I swiftly appraise him of
    the situation.

MARNIE
We hear a

TA DA DADA DA DA-DA!

and Zed uncurls my fingers
from his wrist
so he can let Luca in.

ZED
Luca says his sister has heavy periods.
He sprays lavender water for calm
& presses hot oat bags on
    Marnie's back & belly.
Take the codeine, you idiot, he tells her.
Stop punishing yourself.

MARNIE
I'm sorry! I'm sorry!
I sob onto Luca's shoulder.

I didn't want this baby and
I didn't want to carry it,
but I am really sorry
just the same.

ZED
Luca holds her tight while she cries.
He strokes her back & tells her how brave she is,
that she's doing the right thing.

I'm not sure about the lavender,
but the pain relief, the words & the warmth,
    seem to work.
Gradually Marnie's crying subsides.
Her body uncurls itself as her cramps ease off.

I feel ravaged by the passage of her emotion,
a hurricane-wrecked town.

MARNIE
The painful storm has passed.
It's over.
I'm not pregnant any more.

I go to the bathroom
and stare at my reflection.

Am I a killer?
The law says no.

Am I a killer?
Rakel thinks so.

Am I a killer?
Yes and no.

Chapter Twenty-Seven

ZED
Mother calls up a ten-minute warning.
    Supper's nearly ready. *Everybody out!*

Marnie emerges from my bathroom.
She's been washing her hands
    for longer than Lady Macbeth.
Am I a murderer now? she asks bleakly.

Luca springs up & wraps his long arms around her.
No, mi amor, you are NOT!

Am I, Zed? Marnie's voice is small & muffled.

My research revealed
    a staggering breadth of opinion
    about when a foetus
    becomes a person.

Not all secular sources agree,
& interestingly, neither do religions –
not even among themselves.

They think it could be
    at conception
    or when the nervous system develops
    or when the heart first beats
    or when the mother can feel it kicking
    or forty,
        or ninety,
            or one hundred & twenty,
                or two hundred & twelve
                      days after conception

or when it can live outside the mother's body
> or when it takes its first breath
>> or even when the child first answers 'Amen'.

So really, it's anybody's guess.

But Marnie is waiting to hear
  if *I* think she's a murderer.

I do not believe you are, I tell her.
I personally believe you were only carrying the
  potential *for a human being,*
  if that helps?

She smiles at me, gratefully.
Her hair sticks up,
her face is pale & blotchy.
She looks worse than after Harry's party.

If she doesn't want to tell us who the father was,
that's fine.
It's her business, not mine.

Still, I can't stop thinking how
  it took two people
  to make this baby –

but Marnie's the one bearing
  all of the blame.

MARNIE
Luca walks me to the bus stop
  through the drizzling rain -
   or rather, he pushes me
    perched on his saddle.

My belly still aches.
I feel battered
but relieved.

So, he says, *the way
Zed was helping you . . .
Please tell me
he wasn't the dad?*

Writhing inside
at the echo of my lie,
I shake my head
in denial.

We're at the bus stop.
Luca helps me down from the saddle
more carefully than
I deserve.

Was it Harry then?
he asks.

I'm too
weak and tired
to pretend any more.
My voice stumbles.
*I only slept with him once.
I was drunk. And stupid.*

Luca gently squeezes my hand
and guides me to
the bus queue.

I did wonder, he says.
*As soon as Jessica's text hit the fan,
the cabrón was out there
painting 'Marnie is a slag' on the wall.
He was in such a hurry,
he used ketchup!*

Luca laughs, then
stops when he
sees the look on my face.
He shrugs.
*At least it washed off easy.
Anyway* – he waves his arm for the bus –
*Rakel caught him literally red-handed.
She sent a photo to the senior leadership
and got him a detention.*

Good. I bite my lip.
*Harry was such a mistake.
But I shouldn't have
let Zed take the blame.*

It wasn't your finest hour,
Luca agrees cheerfully.
*But it'll blow over.
Did you tell Harry about the baby?*

The 146 is lumbering up the road towards us.
*I did think about it.
But I knew telling him
would only make him angry –
just give him more ammo against me.*

Harry didn't care about me.
He didn't care about my life
or my feelings
or my future
or my health.

I fumble for my bus pass.
He lied to me.
Do you really think
he deserves
my truth?

Luca shakes his head. He gets it.
Luca, could you . . . I hesitate.
Would you tell Rakel about the . . .
that I had the –
the –
the –

But I can't say it. Not here,
not in the open air, sandwiched
between strangers
waiting for a bus.

Marnie, querida –
Luca grabs my arm –
if you can't even say the word,
how can you face the world?

He steps in close
and holds my shoulders.
*You had an **abortion**,*
he says firmly. *It's not a crime.*
And you're not a horrible person.

The queue shuffles forward.
You don't have to be ashamed, he says to me,
of the decision you had to make.
I think you're very brave.
He kisses me goodbye.

On the bus, I sit hunched
into a corner at the back.
There are ten missed calls from my mum.

Now it's all done,
now I've sorted out my mess,
will I have the courage to confess?

Abortion, I whisper, practising.
I had an abortion.

I watch Luca's red chilli lights
vanishing bravely
into the gloom.

ZED
The dining room has been
    turned into a different world.
Bright with candles. Festive.
On the table there's a wine bucket
    filled with ice & two bottles.
Stacked pizza boxes & a bag of
    garlic dough balls.

I check my watch.
It's not Saturday. So why a takeaway?
Nothing is normal this evening.

MARNIE
At home, a lonely bowl of pasta
sits solidifying
on the kitchen table.

Mum doesn't even wait for me
to sit behind it
before she goes full pit-bull mode,
charging round the kitchen
in her nursing tunic.
*At last! For goodness' sake, where have you **been**?*
Why didn't you pick up when I called?
It's bad enough I had to cook,
but you don't even bother
to eat it?

I
just
close my
eyes, and let
her rant roll over
me. My throat aches.
I want to sit down and
not ever move again.
I let the warm wet
of tears roll down
unchecked.

Marnie?

Marnie?

MARNIE!
Are you listening to me?

Mum's voice changes.
Marnie?
Whatever's the matter?

I open my eyes
and look into hers,
so like mine.

Mum,
I just had an abortion.

She drops a jar of pasta sauce.
It splatters in
bright clots
across the floor.

ZED

My mother's holding the neck of a Prosecco
    in one hand & a two-litre lemonade
    in the other,
triumphant as a racing driver.

How was the revision? she asks, but
    doesn't wait for an answer.
She's beaming,
so unlike her recent self I'm suspicious.
Did I miss an occasion?

We're celebrating! I've kept my job!
You can go to the independent after all!
My mother & I don't hug (that would be weird)
but she pours us each a drink
& we clink our fizzes,
    raising a toast to
    second chances.

However she does seem to have
    entirely overlooked
    one thing.
I messed up the Physics Marathon.
What if I don't get in?

MARNIE
I thought Mum would be so angry with me,
but she's furious with herself.
I knew something was wrong! she says.
Oh, Marnie, my darling, I'm so sorry
you didn't think you could tell me.

With her arms around me now,
I wish I had.
We cry a lot.

We drink hot chocolate and
I say I'm sorry I let her down.
She asks how it happened
and I tell her
the story with Harry
because I need her to know
that I tried to
be careful.

I honestly thought –
I mean, he said –
Mum, I was so stupid.
I was drunk.
I couldn't see
what he was doing:
he tricked me.

Mum's face darkens.
I hear that story a lot, she says,
about boys refusing to wear condoms.
She takes my cup
and carefully puts it
on the table.

*But if you **thought** he was using one –
if that's the sex you
consented to –
Marnie,
did you know that's a crime?
It's called stealthing,
and it's actually,
technically,
rape.*

RAPE?
I nearly choke.

Rape?
The word is a sword
that severs the air between us.
She can't be serious.

*I wasn't raped, Mum!
I said yes – at least at first.
And when I changed my mind,
he stopped.*

Too late, obviously,
says Mum,
crossing her arms
and narrowing her eyes.

But yes, Marnie –
she says, more gently this time,
I couldn't be more serious.

Stealthing is
illegal
as well as
immoral,
unfair,
dangerous
and disrespectful.

She takes my hand and squeezes it.
Do you want to press charges
against him?

WHAT?
I snatch my hand back.
I don't want to press anything
against Harry Borman,
ever again.

No,
I whisper.
I really don't.
Please, don't make me do that.
I just want to get on with my life.
Forget it ever happened.

I think Mum's going to argue –
but she sighs
and starts mopping
the mess of pasta sauce.
Don't forget it, love.
Learn from it.

She looks up at me,
a spiral of hair escaping
from its knot,
and smiles gently.
Like I did.

I tell Mum about taking her
stashed morning after pill
and she twists the tomatoey
dishcloth in her hands.
I wish you'd come to me.
Why didn't you?

I open my mouth to tell her
how bad I felt
that I'd let her down,
but a yawn comes out instead.

She puts me to bed.
Tucks me in like I'm tiny,
gives me all I need
to soothe the pain.

I'm sorry, Mum, about everything,
I say, my body relaxing,
my shell softening,
dissolving.

She kisses my head.
Me too, love.
We'll do better
next time.

ZED
Mother is surprisingly chilled
    when I ask what will happen
    if I don't get in.
We'll cross that bridge
    when it is presented, she says,
as though my future hasn't always been
    micro-planned.
Just get your grades,
   you'll be fine.

Shocker.

I'm glad she didn't
come out with something anodyne like
    Just do your best.

Then I'd *know* the aliens had swapped her.

After supper, I pick up my phone
& without scrolling through the
    hundreds of toxic new messages,
delete the class group socials.

I block a few of the nastier individuals too,
wishing it would wipe
    my private life
        from their minds.

MARNIE
I unblock Rakel.
She must've been trying to reach me because
my phone rings right away.

I answer.
Hi, Rakel.

She sounds relieved.
MARNIE! I've been trying to call you for days.

Uh-huh.

Luca told me what you – what you – what you did.

That word again. I swallow.
I had an abortion, Rakel,
You can say the word
out loud.

Pause.
Um . . . how was it?

Horrible.
But at least it's over.

Another pause.
Well, anyway,
I've been trying to tell you I'm sorry.
I was out of order before.

She really was.

We start talking at the same time.

Maybe I   *You really*
shouldn't have –   *shouldn't have –*
Sorry, go on –   *Sorry, go on –*

                                                           No, you.

Rakel continues.
Luca had a proper go at me, she says.
Made me see
I shouldn't have tried
to tell you what to do.

My religion teaches tolerance,
and I wasn't . . . you know . . . tolerant.
Empathic.
Whatever.

I wanted to say I'm sorry.

                                The back of my throat aches.
                                 You don't hate me now?

Rakel sniffs.
I – well, I wouldn't have done what you did,
but you're not me.

                                          Really not!
                                     I try to lighten up.
                               I hate hockey for starters.

It doesn't work.
I would have kept it,
she says, in a very small voice.

>   I think,
> How can she be so sure
> when it's never happened to *her*?
>   but instead I joke,
> *Well, any baby of yours would be an*
> *immaculate conception, wouldn't it?*
> *A miracle. Like Jesus.*
> *You'd **have** to keep it – think of the media deals!*

>   In the shocked silence,
>   I hear Rakel's gum pop.

Then she gives a little giggle.
I think that might be
blasphemy!

>   I laugh with relief.
> *But seriously, Rakel, people make mistakes,*
>   *and not everyone wants to stay a virgin*
>   *until their wedding night,*
>   *you know?*

Oh, you think that's easy?
There's a flash of anger in her voice
I haven't heard before.
Being called frigid,
being thought a prude?
Having phone porn flashed in my face
because the boys want
a reaction?

She's right. It's tough being a girl.
We're damned if we do,
damned if we don't.

I wish I hadn't said that, I tell her.
I'm sorry.

Another pause.
Me too,
Rakel says softly.
So, are we okay now?

I think about it,
for about quarter of a second.
Yeah.

Chapter Twenty-Eight

ZED	**MARNIE**
One week's holiday left.	**One week's holiday left.**
Where did the time go?	Where did the time go?
The exams start	The exams start
in less than	in less than
three weeks.	three weeks.
I'm behind schedule –	I'm behind schedule –
but no more excuses.	but no more excuses.
Time to roll up my sleeves.	Time to roll up my sleeves.

I've got ink all the way up my arms.
Printing's pretty messy.

I've thrown myself into my *Freedom* project,
developing the ideas for
prints in my portfolio.
But I want to mash up
the media, add videos into
the mix.

I'm asking,
What does freedom mean to you?

I want my work to do something.
I want it to provoke thought,
change minds.

Maybe make up
for my mistakes.

ZED

I'm sure there are picnic places
    more picturesque than this.
We're looking out
    at the playing fields
    beside the Wall of Words.
Marnie invited us here &
    the caretaker let us in –
It's odd being here with no one else around.

Rakel's not impressed.
She's loaded with steel tiffin boxes
    packed by her mum.
Can't we go by the river?

Put them down. We'll eat later, says Marnie.
I brought a blanket.
She might, in fact, have bought a duvet:
her rucksack is enormous.

How the heck
    did you get them to let us in?
says Luca, kicking a can so hard it
    bounces off an expletive on the wall.

Naomi swung it for me, Marnie says.
They're going to paint the wall tomorrow.
This is my last chance.

I hate this wall.
Luca is staring at

Luca is a fag!

   splashed onto the brick.
I'm glad they're painting it,
but it's just whitewash.
All this crap
   will be back by summer.
It always is.

Not if I can help it, says Marnie,
pulling a telescopic tripod
   from her bag.
I want you all to think
   what this wall represents.
Tell me what you want to be free from.
She waves the tripod at the wall.
You can choose your own backdrop.

MARNIE
They take a moment to catch on.

When they do,
Zed blushes like
I've asked him to strip
butt-naked.

Luca looks thoughtful
and asks to think for a moment –

but Rakel straight away
slots herself in front of
an enormous pair of
crudely drawn disembodied breasts
labelled with her name.

No prizes for guessing who the artist was.

*Looks like Harry got payback
for that detention,*
says Luca grimly.

I set the video rolling
and we begin.

Rakel wants
the freedom to be a *girl*.
She wants the right to play hockey, do homework,
watch Pixar, giggle at stupid jokes,
have boys just as friends.

She's sick of her boobs being leered at
or touched up on the bus.
She wants to grow up at her own pace.
It's not a lot to ask, she says.
*Since when was
staying a virgin
until your wedding night
a crime?*

ZED
Luca's up next. He peruses the wide range of
    homophobic insults
before he picks a particularly
    poisonous backdrop for his piece.

Marnie frames him with her phone.
Go on then, Luca, she says.
Tell us how freedom should feel.

Luca flicks his fringe out of his eyes.
You know, I've never let anyone see
    how much I hate this . . . hate speech.
He points to the slurs smeared on the wall.

I never wanted to give those –
    he hunts for a word
    & settles on Spanish – **idiotas** –
    the satisfaction of reaction.
But of course it hurts.

I want every young kid
    to be free
        to express & explore
            their sexuality.

He steps closer to the camera,
his face uncharacteristically uncertain.
I guess I'm sorry now
    I haven't put up a fight
    to protect the ones
    who haven't got the armour,
the ones who can't run fast enough
    from the meatheads . . .

His voice falters. He swallows.
Maybe I can do that now, like this.

I confess I'm surprised.
I'd assumed Luca was invulnerable.

Marnie points at me.
Your turn now.
This is most unfair.
She lured me here with a litre of Coke,
& now she wants me to
>   expose myself
>   on video.

Do I really have to?

Luca pokes me.
Stick up for yourself, Zed! he says.
*They should stop trying to tag you
>   with their labels.*

Labels . . . That gives me an idea.
I pull my paper face mask & a Sharpie from my pocket
& scribble a plea
>   for my anonymity.

I stay stock-still & speechless
while Marnie makes a
>   short,
>   silent
>   movie.

MARNIE
After Zed's speechless protest
I ask Luca to
film me.

I speak up about
reproductive freedom,
the right for women to make
their own choices
without fear,
without violence.

I talk of a dream world without
coercion,
judgement
or
stigmatisation,
but
I know the lens can also see
so many words that want
to shame me
and
it's hard
to hold my head up.

ZED	**MARNIE**
Marnie plays the films back.	**I play the films back.**
They're pretty good,	They're pretty good,
even mine.	even mine.

You were amazing, guys, thanks!
I tell them.
They were brilliant, really,
even Zed.

I know I kind of sprang that on you –
but I didn't want you to
waste time preparing,
or get stressed.
I wanted you to be real.

I bend
to pack stuff away
so no one notices
my tears.

ZED
We pretend we don't see
Marnie getting emotional.

Rakel picks up her tiffin boxes.
If you're done fixing the world, Marnie,
can we please go somewhere nice
to have this picnic?

MARNIE
Back home, I cut those films super-fast.
Naomi says I can play the interviews
as talking heads on screens.

My GSCE exam is going to be
the most polarising,
political,
exciting,
innovative,
activistic,
original,
important
art project
Downham has ever seen.

MARNIE
It's nearly midnight, Marnie!
calls Mum.
You should be asleep.
She comes into my room
and looks over my shoulder.

I'm planning the screen-printed posters
to accompany the films.
What do you think? I ask Mum,
suddenly anxious.

She lays a soft hand on my shoulder.
I think they're amazing.
I've got a super-talented,
very resourceful,
very brave daughter.

There's a smile in her voice.
And I'm very proud of you.

Chapter Twenty-Nine

ZED
On the last day of the
   Easter holidays,
I'm round at Marnie's,
on the floor of her bedroom,
   surrounded by packaging from
   post-Easter food-bank chocolate eggs.
We're revising chemistry. My blood sugar's off the scale.

The abortion kit is open on her bed.
Marnie sees me looking at the opened STI test box.
I got the results today. All clear, thank God.

I pick up the leaflet & read it.
Weren't Chlamydia & Gonorrhoea
   the daughters of King Lear?

I have to
   duck the pillow
   Marnie chucks.

MARNIE
Mum says the rate of STIs is soaring
because young people don't use condoms.
   She says, if Harry's sleeping around

unprotected

there's a really good chance
he'll get infected one day
and pass it on like an
unwelcome gift.

> *You can have chlamydia without even knowing,*
> *I tell Zed.*
> *It can make you infertile.*

ZED
I look up from my phone.
I hear it kills koalas.

> **MARNIE**
> *Really?*
> *Well, they should use condoms too.*

ZED
Given the risks, the mess,
& the existence of artificial insemination,
I honestly can't think why anyone
   indulges in sexual intercourse.

After a moment, Marnie says –

> **MARNIE**
> *Zed?*

ZED
Yes?

> **MARNIE**
> ***You know who got me pregnant,***
> ***don't you?***

ZED
I'm reasonably confident I do, yes.
But it's not my business.

MARNIE
Thank you.

I fiddle with one of the condoms
from the bento box.
*Just so you know,
I wasn't a total idiot.
I gave him a condom, but
he only pretended to use it.*

ZED
He what?
It takes a moment for the
    sheer asinine,
        arrogant
            cruelty of this
to sink in.
My opinion of Harry
    shrinks to a
    subatomic
    scale.

MARNIE
*Mum says that's stealthing, and it's illegal.
She says it's actually rape.*

ZED
I quickly
    verify this on my phone.
It's true.

MARNIE
Look, I don't want to get Harry
arrested or anything –
I don't want to even
think about him ever again –
but he needs to know
it's not okay,
don't you think?

I hope Zed gets the hint.

ZED
Marnie looks at me
somewhat awkwardly.

I study her face.
I think she might be telling me
it's my business
after all.

MARNIE
A bit later, when we've
moved from revising biology to maths,
a message from Rakel arrives in the group chat.

She wants to go ice skating.

> last day of freedom!
> why don't we all
> go together?

ZED
I'm first to reply.

> Because ice skating is a really inefficient, potentially dangerous method of travelling to somewhere you have no real desire to go?

> shut up zed!

> shut up zed!

> shut up zed!

Apparently we're going.

MARNIE
The ice rink's in Zone 6,
so we travel by Tube.
It used to be a cinema,
still says *The Roxy* on the sign outside.

Luca and Rakel are waiting for us in the foyer,
where a ghost smell of popcorn
clings to the carpet.

ZED
Inside the rink
K-pop bounces off the shiny ice.
I, unfortunately, do not.

I'm glad I wore my army helmet,
but every fall still hurts.

MARNIE
I'm laughing at Zed so hard my sides hurt.
He looks like a newborn giraffe.

Meanwhile,
Luca glides languid as a panther.
Rakel waddles fast like a determined duck.
And me? I'm a snake, wiggling backwards.
We spend a lot of time laughing.

After a while, I leave them
to hunt for the loos.
I'm still bleeding a bit –
Sherana said that's perfectly normal –
and I need to change my pad.

The toilets smell of the rubber
anti-slip matting
and echo with the laughter
of a cluster of girls
lacing up their blades.

One cackle brings the hairs up
on my neck.
I back out quickly –
but not before Jessica Bates
spots me in the mirror.

Oy! Pregga! Slag!
she yells in a voice
loud enough to crack ice.

I freeze.

Look, girls, she calls to her cronies,
it's the baby mama!

I force myself to face her.
Is this what my life
will be from now on?
Forever shamed by people like
Jessica Bates?

We lock eyes,
and anger begins
its slow rise in my body,
tingling up through my legs
my belly, my chest, my head –
until I'm breathing out
a red-hot spark
of resolution.

Today I'm not having it.
I'm not taking this.

Today it stops.

Jessica, I say,
breathing deep,
keeping my face impassive,
looking straight into her spidery eyes.
I want to talk to you about Harry.
In private, please.
I have something to say
you won't want other people to hear.

Jessica Bates
looks me up and down
and something must tell her I mean it.

All right, girls, she says,
and waves them away
with an airy hand.
I'll call you if I need you.

They wobble out,
shaky on their blades.

She knows, I think.

For the first time,
I feel something like pity.
It creeps in under the hate.
What must it be like
to be with someone like Harry,
so slippery you have to chain him?

I tell Jessica the simple truth.
That I slept with her boyfriend, just once,
when we were both drunk.

But once was enough,
because he lied
when he implied
he had the contraception
under control.

I say I'm sorry.
God knows I *am* sorry.
I couldn't be sorrier.

She studies her nails.
Why should I believe you? she says,
but her voice is uncertain.
You're making it up.

I tell her about the Andrew Tate poster,
Harry's freckled shoulders,
the cheesy music track he played.

From her silence, from the way she bites her lip,
I think I've hit home.

Then I show her a picture of the bento box
as proof I'm not pregnant
any more.

Jessica, I say,
*this doesn't make
either of us look good.
I don't want anyone to know
I slept with your skanky boyfriend either.*

She narrows her eyes
but I ignore my pulse of fear
because this is my one chance
to fix the mess I made.

I try to keep the shake
out of my voice.
*So you've got to pretend
you were just joking
about me being pregnant,
okay?
I mean it.
If you don't want me to
neon-paint the truth
about your boyfriend
on the wall,
you've got to make them all believe
you were just trash-talking
about me and Zed.*

She steps toward me and
I grip the basin behind for support.

Jessica Bates puts her face
close to mine,
and I wait for the threat –

but she breathes out
a long-drawn-out
peppermint-flavoured
Okaaaaay.

>   But when
>   I make the mistake
>   of suggesting
>   she gets herself checked
>   for an infection,
>   she freaking *explodes.*

>   Given how Jessica Bates
>   reacted to a case of nits,
>   I should have known.

>   I get out
>   before she stabs me
>   with her mascara wand.

ZED
After Marnie tells me
   what happened in the toilets,
I unblock Harry Borman.
It will be an unpleasant but necessary contact,
rather like picking up dog poo.

> I know what you did to Marnie.
> It was *stealthing*. It's a crime.

> Marnie has the right to get
> you arrested for rape.

> So I wouldn't make any plans for the summer, if I were you.

> Risking a sexually transmitted infection isn't cool either.

> Just ask Jessica.

The response that comes back is
    really quite abusive,
so I tell him where to go
    in two economical words.

Then I re-block him quickly before
holstering my smoking phone
    with – I admit –
        some satisfaction.

Chapter Thirty

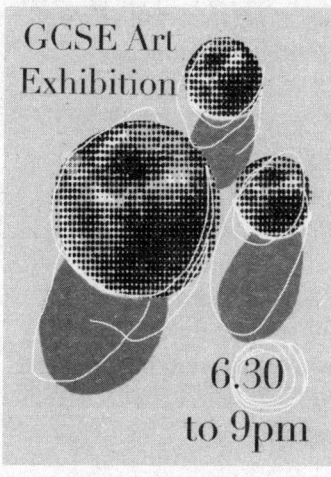

MARNIE
The next day, summer term begins.
We even haven't got to registration
before Jessica and Harry are
yelling at each other
outside the science block
like they're in the ring,
no holds barred.

ZED
I look on from a discreet distance.

Jessica has Harry in a metaphorical armlock.
You even spread that stupid rumour
 about Marnie & Zed! she yells,
her angry face
 kissing-close to his.
Just because she wouldn't let you
 into her pants! You're pathetic!

Marnie said Jessica had agreed,
but I was expecting a quiet retraction –
some post somewhere relieving me of shame.

Shifting the blame to Harry
 is way more
 than I could have hoped for.

Jessica is winning the fight –
she's better armed & faster with her comebacks,
landing jealous jabs & caustic crosses
 until Harry is on the ropes.

I do, of course, deplore violence –
but waged in words, it's fun to watch.

Jessica finishes with a blow below the belt:
D'you know what else? You're a crap shag.
I faked it. Every. Single. Time!
The circling crowd whoops & yells.

MARNIE
Harry Borman stamps by,
    mate-less and castrated.
    He glares at me.
    I smile sweetly.

News, both real and fake, is ripped to shreds;
    fact and fiction pulped together,
        headlines blowing past me
            just like litter.

Break time,
    I'm the centre of attention again.

Is it true Harry Borman just made it all up?

So you're not really pregnant?

    I laugh.
    What do you think?

I tell them they really should
    interrogate their sources.
That rumour about Zed ... *seriously?*

ZED
A few kids come
& apologise awkwardly
   for the things they said on socials.

What things? I ask guilelessly,
& relish how they can't
   repeat their insults to my face.

I'm glad this is out of the way.
Now perhaps I can get on with my GCSEs.

MARNIE
In art, it's all about the exam.
While Mr Challoner balances bananas
in a bowl of boring fruit,
I show Naomi a picture of
the postcard I made for Zed.

It's great! she says.

I tell her how I learned to
control the drag by trial and error.
I confess my first prints
were rubbish – I wasted most
of the paper she left me.

Naomi shrugs.
Don't worry about it.
You gotta make mistakes
or else you don't learn.

She says she'll help all she can.

We have to hand our coursework in today.
Mr Challoner looks puzzled at my portfolio
& positively *pales*
when he views the videos.

He calls Naomi into his office
for a talk.

ZED
Another Marnie drama.
The art teacher thinks her project is
    too **bold**
        too RADICAL,
            too *far out*
                to pass.

He wants to rein her in to something safer,
less polemic.

But the art tech disagrees.
Just go for it, she told Marnie outside the room,
where the teacher couldn't hear.

MARNIE
Naomi said Mr Challoner can't stop me.
And even if he marks me down,
she bets the moderators won't.

She says my work ticks all the boxes
required for the top grade. It's definitely a
*personal and meaningful response that
realises intentions and demonstrates
understanding of visual language.*

It's also risky.

But Naomi says real artists take risks,
and my work is *important*.
It will get people thinking.

I just need to be brave, she says.

ZED
The morning of Marnie's art exam,
I am afraid for her, a sick pit
of fear in my stomach.

I remember the way I felt at Oxford,
with my life held
in the palm of a few
short hours.

MARNIE
The art exam lasts two whole days:
five long hours each day.
But I'll still have to work quickly.

On day one
I prepare the posters.

I separate the colours,
print the acetates,
mask and emulsion the screens,
peg them up to dry overnight.

I set up four computer monitors on plinths,
tacking down the trailing cables
to stop moderators breaking their necks
before they've boosted my marks.

Our talking heads face each other
across my screened-off section:
Rakel, Luca, Zed and me,
having a close-captioned conversation.

I finish just as Mr Challoner
tells us to lay down our brushes.

So? says Mum at home,
handing me a
heart-attack-sized flapjack.
How did it go?

But I just grin.
I don't want to speak
too soon.

On day two
I screen-print the
protest posters, and
they come out really well –
not perfect, but a big improvement
on their predecessors.

I pin each poster
on the speaker plinths,
to summarise
what we're saying.

The last piece of my installation
is what Naomi calls *realia* –
real objects to enable learning.

I mount the abortion bento box
on its own grim plinth.
Mr Challoner walks past and sniffs,
but I'm concentrating
too hard to care.

And in the final fifteen minutes
I blow up the condoms
and pose them in naughty positions.
There. That should properly
piss him off.

Time's up!

I step back.
Kind of to my surprise,
my GCSE art exam just went
exactly how I'd planned.

Outside the art room,
Naomi cheers and slaps a high five.
*You did it! You're using your art
to make change!*

I hope I am.
I don't know if it will
please the examiners, but
I'm proud of what I've produced.

I want to make amends –

to Mum,

to my butter bean.

Chapter Thirty-One

ZED **Study leave begins.** Mother sticks my exam timetable to the fridge. We tick the papers off one by one. *You're doing fine*, she says, & feeds me kale.	**MARNIE** **Study leave begins.** Mum sticks my exam timetable to the fridge. We tick the papers off one by one. *You're doing fine,* she says, and feeds me cake.

ZED
Day one of GCSEs.

Marnie & I are
    outside the exam hall
    clutching our clear pencil cases,
waiting for the (walkover of) Physics Paper One.

Mother has become most unpredictable,
I tell Marnie. *This morning she announced that,*
    since I didn't get into the summer school –

Sorry about that, mutters Marnie,
    for, I believe,
    the fifty-first time –

we're going on a trip to CERN!
I'm unable to keep the excitement
    from my voice. *I'll actually see
the Large Hadron Collider!*

The Large Hadron what? says Marnie,
checking for the sixth time that
    her calculator is working.

I roll my eyes. My friend's general knowledge
    has some serious   gaps.
*Collider! Only the most powerful
particle accelerator ever built!*

Wow, says Marnie, not sounding like she means it.

MARNIE
Whatever floats his boat.
Personally I'd rather go to Ibiza,
but the chances of that are
microscopic.

Zed is totally *super-charged* about his trip:
he's firing words and phrases at me
at the speed of light,
while
I'm trying to remember if
momentum = mass × velocity
or if it's the other way around.

Ionising particle ... dark matter ... dark energy ... blah blah ... antimatter matter ... Higgs boson ... origin of mass particle ... blah blah ... 13.8 billion years ... blah blah ... accelerator ... synchrocyclotron ... nanoscience ... magnetic monopoles ... blah blah ... Big Bang ... blah ... high-speed collision ... gravity supersymmetry ... Standard Model ... data ... blah ... gravitons ... fourth dimension ... theory of relativity ... photons ... quantum computing ... blah ... microscopic black holes ... teraelectron volt ... quark-gluon plasma ... decay ... superconduction ... muons ...

Blah blah blah blah blah.
On and on and on
he goes,
nonsense words colliding with the
utter panic at my core.

I don't even try to listen,
just breathe deeply
and try to keep
it together.

My mind is a vacuum.
I can't remember a single formula.
How can I get the grade Mum wants?
A *six* feels like a physical
impossibility.

ZED
I notice
>how miserable Marnie looks –

which is a borderline insult to my physics teaching,
but I'll let it go.
I stop talking about CERN.

MARNIE
>**Zed stops talking.**
>He puts his skinny arm
>around my shoulders.
>*Don't worry*, he says. *You'll be fine.*
>
>I know
>he can't tolerate touch,
>but that hug really helped.

ZED
There's the usual exit poll as we file out of the hall.
I measure Marnie's answers against my own:
she actually did quite well, considering
>how difficult
>everyone else thinks it was.

It seems better not to mention
>I've found walks in the park
>considerably more challenging.

For the Spanish listening paper
I take a leaf from Marnie's book.
When I'm not sure which box
>to tick, I pick a number from
>the three repeating digits
at the end of the Collatz sequence.

I choose *1*
    then *4*
        then 2
            then *1*
                then *4*
                    then 2 . . .

There is a statistical probability of 99.86%
    that at least one answer
    will be correct.

Scarily, all Mother said this morning
    was, *Do your best.*

I do truly believe she's been
    body-snatched.

MARNIE
After the Spanish oral, we snatch snacks.
Zed munches his way through
three Lion bars before speaking.
Well, that was a great big –
he Google-translates –
montón de mierda, was it not?

It was not, actually. It was easy,
and the second test I know I've passed today:
this morning my double-check
pregnancy test was
reassuringly negative.

           Luca stretches out his arms to Zed
               in a consolation air-hug,
                    but surprisingly
                     Zed's smiling,
                         chilled.

ZED
Six weeks later
(41 days, 22 hours & fifty-one minutes to be precise)
the exams are done.

It's all over.

                                    MARNIE
                         It might be all over for Zed,
                                but I've still got the
                                GCSE art exhibition.

                       The art show's kind of a big deal.

                   After the moderators have been and
                                        (I hope)
                            moderated the heck out of
                                Mr Challoner's grade,
                              the school shows off
                                  its creativity
                                 with a big *Wow!*
                              Aren't we wonderful?
                            display in the art block.

Naomi says loads of people come,
and not just from Downham.
The sixth-form college
art department
will be there
for sure.

That's why I love art, I say to Zed.
*There's nothing beautiful
about the GCSE physics papers,
is there?*

ZED
I quote Melvin Schwartz, Nobel prize winner
& discoverer of the muon neutrino:
*The beauty of physics
   lies in the extent [to] which
   seemingly complex unrelated phenomena
   can be explained & correlated
   through a high level of abstraction
   by a set of laws
   which are amazing in their simplicity.*

MARNIE
Zed says something.

Then he pulls out his phone
and shows me a picture of
the Large Hadron Collider.
It looks more like
a Large Drainage Pipe
running through a Tube tunnel.

Nice, I say.

Chapter Thirty-Two

ZED
Downham doesn't do
a prom,
thank goodness.

MARNIE
Downham doesn't do
a prom,
thank goodness.

Hopefully there'll be no more parties
with Harry Borman ever:
the art exhibition
will draw a line
under the painful sentence
that was Downham High.

But as the private view gets closer,
I get more and more
uncomfortable.

I asked my friends
to free themselves from shame,
to go on the record –
but I was too scared
to tell the truth
myself.

Why?
Why did I
ask Jessica to lie?
Why did I pretend
the pregnancy didn't happen?

After all,
the choice I had to make
was forced upon me
by Harry's words.

His *I got this covered* kept me in the dark.
Harry's stealth removed my consent.

I did
what was
right for me,
but it made me feel
so ashamed.

The night before the exhibition
I lie awake for ages
feeling bad about
not being brave enough.

And what about Jessica,
twisted up with jealousy,
insecurity and need?
The way she was shaded
makes her Harry's victim too.

I go into the bathroom
and turn on the light.

Who are you, Marnie Staedler?
My reflection stares back at me:
straggly plaits snaking
over my shoulders,
snarled rivulets of indecision.
Long hair
Harry said he loved.

Naomi said artists must be brave –
but she had no idea
just how brave
I'm going to be.

I pick up the nail scissors.

Marnie, it's the middle of the night!
Mum walks into the
brightly lit bathroom
just as I *snip!*
the last of my braids
and

i

t

d
r
o
p
s

to join the
tangle at my feet.

Oh! Mum gasps.
What have you done?

I put down the scissors
and take a look at the
new, clear-eyed, *braver* me
staring back from the glass.
Hair cropped short, no fringe,
nothing to hide behind.

A style that says:
No shame here.

But perhaps it is a bit more
scruffy than I'd planned . . .
Mum, I say,
a little help here?

Mum draws in a breath.
I'll do what I can, she says, smiling,
and picks up the shears.

We talk while she
tidies up the tufts,
talk about the choices
I can make now.
It's gone 2 a.m.
before we're finished.

I go back to bed, and this time
sleep takes me
fast as shutdown.

When I message Jessica the next morning,
I'm hoping she's still hopping mad.
It turns out I'm in luck:
nobody can hold a grudge
like Jessica Bates.

Yeah, Harry hates using condoms.
By eleven o'clock
Jessica's sitting at my kitchen table
in front of a pack of custard creams.

He made me go on the pill,
even though it makes me fat.
He said I had to diet.
She stirs three sugars into her tea.

He said it was my fault
he fooled around with other girls.
He said I was too clingy:
he felt trapped.
He said I was lucky to have him at all.

She looks up and catches my expression.
But he always came back, you know?
He'd bring me presents and everything,
to say he was sorry.

I pass her a biscuit.
She glares at me.
At least I never knew who they were –
not until you.

Didn't you worry about
any other . . . presents
he might have brought you?
I ask, thinking of those
two daughters of King Lear.

But Jessica thinks only dirty girls get diseases.
Anyway, she got her test back
and she's not a dirty girl.

Harry's had a lot of luck then, I say.
I fetch another
pack of custard creams.

Jessica's brain was so thoroughly
washed, it takes real work
(and a shit ton of biscuits)
to deprogramme her.

But finally, she believes me
that good girls get infections too,
and love shouldn't make you
feel like crap.

Now she wants to punch Harry
for real,
but
I tell her
we can do
so much better than that.

We can show him
how much
humiliation hurts.

Jessica, I say,
*would you like to
take part in a protest?*

I offer her
a brand-new
arsenal of words
to use as weapons:
*disrespected, gaslit, coerced, pressured,
blackmailed, belittled, forced –*
and best of all,
empowered.

By the time we start filming,
she's firing on all guns.

Afterwards
there's an awkward goodbye
on the doorstep.

We don't hug.

Jessica Bates and I
will never be friends,
but I think after today
we might be
on the same side.

ZED
Are-you-coming? Are-you-coming? Are-you-coming?
Marnie's texts have been buzzing like a
    mosquito in my ear
    all afternoon, &
    now she's calling.

I sigh & give up my attempt to build a
    Minecraft version of the Hadron Collider.
I assume you mean to your exhibition tonight.
You know art's not really my thing, Marnie.

Rakel & Luca will be there!
There's something like desperation
    in her voice.
Please come too.
I need you.

Actually, my reluctance is less a dislike of art
& more a discomfort
    about my own
    onscreen
    exposure.

If I must, I say.

MARNIE
The art room is locked.
It's still hours until the opening,
and only Naomi is here,
adding labels to the displays.
I knock at the door.

She lets me in and whistles.
Wow, nice haircut!
Having one last check?

I nod, guilt nipping my smile in tight.

My circle of heads faces inwards,
already murmuring to each other in low voices,

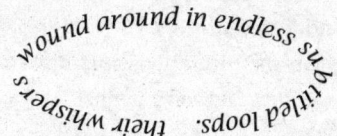

wound around in endless subtitled loops, their whispers

Our scripts play across the screen
to underscore our meaning,
make sure it isn't lost.

Keep the volume low.
Don't want to disturb people,
Mr Challoner said –
but actually, disturbing people
is exactly
what I want to do.

My portfolio – a huge photo album
full of iterative images, sketches and notes –
all my ideas around *Freedom* –
lies open on a table in the middle,
for visitors to flick through.

While Naomi's back is to me,
I pull an envelope out of my pocket.
This won't take long.

ZED
The room's almost full when I arrive.
Luca & Rakel wave me over.
Marnie's here, with a woman
   I presume to be her mother.

Luca whistles. *¡Que guapa!*
Indeed, Marnie's
   unfashionably short hairstyle
   suits her very well.

Marnie's looking worried; she's chewing on her lip.
It's understandable she's tense –
it's her first exhibition.

Actually, we're all nervous,
we're all on show,

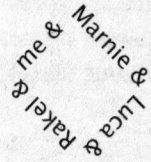

but Marnie is extra,
> **extra**
>> edgy.
The press are coming!
  & the mayor! she whispers.

Jessica's all dressed up like it's the
   Jessica Bates show.
I've no idea why she's here.

We've seen Marnie's work already,
so Rakel & Luca wander among
   the crowd of parents, teachers & students,
   looking at the other pieces.

Nothing as good as Marnie's! Rakel reports back.
She didn't invite her parents along.
They wouldn't understand, she says apologetically.
I don't want to upset them.

Marnie's mother
   squeezes her daughter's hand quickly
& whispers in her ear.

MARNIE
That's the journalist!
Mum whispers.
She points at a frizzy-haired woman
in a bright blue jacket.

Last night
I told Mum what I was planning:
I didn't want to embarrass her.
She laughed.
How could this embarrass me?
You're my poster child!
It was her idea to call the press.

Mr Challoner leads the journalist
to my display. He looks reluctant.
The mayor –
a willowy Black woman wearing
a very chunky chain –
comes too.

I want to pass out / wet myself / run away,
but I don't do any of those things.
I just stand in a corner and
grip Mum's hand tightly.

They're picking the Post-its I inserted
out of the portfolio.
I can't read them from here,
but I don't need to.
I know the lines by heart.

I also swapped the flash drive on my plinth
when Naomi wasn't looking.

There's a new loop on it now:
Jessica's testimonial
spliced with different
words from me.

My heart is jumping,
blood is thudding
in my ears.
Be brave.

Mum squeezes my hand.
Go on, love, now!

Using the remote control,
I select the other file,
turn the volume up high,
and press
play.

Fading in from black
my solemn face stares
from its newly shorn frame,
reciting the same story
sandwiched between the pages
of my portfolio.

*My name is Marnie Staedler
and I'm sixteen years old.
Last month I had an abortion
because my whole life is ahead of me
and being a single parent
isn't what I've planned.*

The word
abortion
slices through
the room:
a murmur
ripples around
like a shockwave.

I have their attention.

My talking head tells them,
*I made a mistake
but I tried to put it right.*

A crowd gathers and watches
as Jessica's face
replaces
mine.

Jessica:
*My name is Jessica Bates
and I made a mistake.
I went out with a boy
who refused
to use
a condom.*

Me:
*I went with a boy
who tricked me into thinking
I was protected
when I was too drunk
to be in control.*

Jessica:
This boy controlled me.
He messed around
with other girls,
and that messed around
with my head.

            Me:
      He let me think he used a condom,
               but he lied.

Jessica:
He tried
to make everything
my fault.

            Me:
          My pregnancy
           was his fault
              but
      the problem we created
           was all mine.

Jessica:
He said every single problem
was mine: he said I was
too jealous, too needy,
too fat, too frigid.

He said no one else
would ever want me –
and I was scared
to be alone.

Me:
*The decision was
mine alone
to make.*

It was so hard.

Jessica:
*When I decided
to ditch him, I found out
being on my own
wasn't so hard.
I'm sorry I didn't
do it before.*

Me:
*I am so, so sorry for
my little butter bean –
but I don't believe
I'm the one
who should be
ashamed.*

Jessica:
*So shame on him!
I'm not allowed to
name names –
but you know who it is.*

Me:
*If you know someone like him,
Don't let them get away with it.*

The screen goes black.

Mr Challoner's face goes purple.
Marnie Staedler!
he shouts.
IS MARNIE STAEDLER HERE?

ZED
Oh, my.
Oh, my friend Marnie.
Oh, my friend Marnie, what have you done?

The mayor stops smiling &
  turns the pages of the portfolio
  with a frown furrowed onto her face.
The journo in the purple jacket
  reaches for a notepad & pen.

Mr Challoner looks around the room
  & calls out, *Marnie Staedler!*
IS MARNIE STAEDLER HERE?

MARNIE
In the small art office
Mum, Mr Challoner, Naomi and me
are all breathing the same air
rather rapidly.

Naomi looks shocked and nervous
but also proud.
She catches my eye and
secretly
winks.

Mr Challoner's rabbity little face
flickers between outrage and fear.

Why is this man an art teacher?
He only wants us to paint
bowls of apples – but
still lives
don't
change lives.

Mum's arm is round my shoulders.

Mr Challoner actually quivers.
You have bought shame to the school!

I'm about to explain it's the opposite –
I want to rid the school of shame –
when there's a *tap-tap-tap* at the door.
Framed in its glass square,
the journalist and the mayor
are applauding.

They open the door a crack.
Is this the artist?
May we have a word?

ZED
Marnie says the art tech was amazingly gracious & let Mr Challoner take all the credit.

Chapter Thirty-Three

Downham High School

Season: Summer
Name: Marnie Staedler
Candidate number:

0033

Results

ZED
Today is Results Day.

Rakel's in India with her family
& Luca's in Spain with his,
so it's just Marnie & me
    meeting by the gates.

I only got back from CERN last night:
it was as exciting
    as I'd hoped.

MARNIE
I hope Harry's not here.

A steady stream of students
files in through the gate,
going in empty-handed and
coming out with a precious envelope
clutched to their chests.

Like ants moving eggs from a nest,
I tell Zed.

ZED
Marnie is misinformed.
Ants don't move eggs,
they move pupae.

MARNIE
For heaven's sake!
Sometimes you can be so pedantic.
I nudge him.
Ped-ANT-ic. Geddit?

ZED
Hilarious. But incorrect.
I permit myself a smile –
*I'm **always** pedantic.*

MARNIE
I roll my eyes.

ZED
It's so hot,
sweat prickles under the Pikachu earmuffs
   I only wore to make her laugh.

MARNIE
I pretend not to notice Zed's earmuffs
so he'll have to keep them on.

It's boiling and I'm scared.
I need a *nine* in art, but
what if the moderators
thought I was too . . .
immoderate?
What if I flunked physics?

It's noisy.
Kids are shouting
and jumping on each other's backs.

Jessica Bates walks past with her parents.

ZED
I find myself waving unironically
at Jessica Bates & wishing her luck.

Like an afterthought,
she waves back.

MARNIE
There's something
I'd like to say to Jessica.

On second thoughts, I'll text her:

> fyi nits much prefer *clean* hair
> so you're good on that too

There's no sign of Harry.

ZED
Harry Borman plans to
   pursue his petrol-head dreams
   at the tech in the next town.
I doubt our paths will cross again.
No one wants him here.

Omar walks by with his parents,
looking nervous, as well he might.

MARNIE
It's a bit late for luck for Omar,
but we wish him it anyway.
I forgot to bring water.
My throat's dry from fear.

Let's get this over with.

ZED
Marnie & I walk through the gate.

Whoa! Where's the –

MARNIE
– wall gone?

Bloody hell, it's vanished.
The whole, libellous, unlovely length of it.

Gone.

ZED
Where the Wall of Words once was
is now a row of planted sticks
that'll be a hedge
  one day.

MARNIE
Wow!
Graffiti-proof.
Genius.

ZED
We head for the hall & pick up our envelopes,
say *hi* to Ms Rahman,
& are ticked off the list.

So that's it. After all these years of
    being processed through the
    statutory school system,
to be shat out without a
    handshake.

Marnie & I stand awkwardly in the atrium.
Around us, students are
    ripping open their results.
Some are crying with joy,
some are just crying.

                                          MARNIE
                                  I look at my envelope.
                                This isn't an ant anything.
                                    It's a hand grenade
                                    with the pin pulled out.

ZED
It feels like everybody's
    baring themselves in public.

Can we go somewhere private
    to do this? I ask Marnie.

                                            MARNIE
                                    Before I can answer,
                                    I hear my name called.

Marnie! I was looking out for you!
Naomi's hurrying over,
her huge halo of hair
pulled back with a bright band.
Scarlet hoops dangle from her ears.

She blinks at Zed's yellow earmuffs.
Interesting.
Shakes herself.

Anyway, Marnie – she waves a bangled arm
at the screen on the far wall –
what d'you think?

ZED
The big screen in the atrium usually scrolls though
   information & admonishments,
      detentions, club notices & successes.

Normally it's just wallpaper,
but today, Marnie's posters are playing
   one by one,
         huge &
               brightly glowing.

MARNIE
I stare, open-mouthed.

Cool, huh?
says Naomi.
*After a bit of persuasion
the senior leadership team agreed
these posters align just fine
with our school values.*

> She hugs me tightly.
> She smells sweaty and warm.
> *I wanted it to be a surprise –*
> *I hope you don't mind?*

> I can't speak. *Mind?*
> They look amazing.

ZED
Actually, *I* minded,
but I signed the permission slip anyway,
& now I'm glad I did.
Marnie looks like
    she's going to burst with happiness.

I, however, hope to never
    see that screen again.

MARNIE
Naomi nods at the screen
then flicks a glittery fingernail
against the envelope in my hand.
Nice legacy, eh?

Does she mean . . . ? Does she know . . . ?

> I grab Zed's arm.
> *Come with me!*

ZED
Marnie drags me towards the
    totally-gender-separated girls' toilets,
& bundles me into the
    third cubicle on the left.

She sits, I stand.
She points at the graffiti on the door.
I see our names & wince.
Marnie rummages in her tatty bag.

MARNIE
I had a little plan,
in case today was my last chance.

ZED
Out comes a paintbrush & a small bottle
labelled *permanent printer's ink*.

MARNIE
The ink's a bit messy, but it does the job.
I didn't want that libel
up there any more,
I say.
Especially if we're not here
to defend ourselves.

I look at the envelope
lying on my lap
& stroke it gingerly.

That's the question, isn't it?
Will we be here
next year?

ZED
Well, there's only one way
to answer that one.
Ready?

ZED
We each slide our thumb
under the flap.

MARNIE
We each slide our thumb
under the flap.

This is it.

It's not the first time
I've been in this cubicle,
heart thudding, feeling sick,
waiting for a result.

Wait, Zed!
I want to
lengthen the fuse
on my unexploded bomb.
Here.

ZED
From that capacious beatnik bag
Marnie pulls a homemade scrapbook,
 its cardboard covers
  tightly tied with twine.

For you, she says. *I made it.*

MARNIE
I made it, **I tell him.**

I wanted to practise different techniques
for my college portfolio,
so I created a book of numbers
which tell the story
of me and Zed.

ZED
I flick through the pages of
    illustrated digits.
Now, this is *my* kind of art.

Thank you,
I say, and I mean it.
Now stop procrastinating.

MARNIE
Zed picks up his envelope again.

I can't bear to open mine.
What will I do if I've failed?

Hey Zed,
what will you do if you don't
get into your posh sixth form?
Don't tell me you haven't
made a spreadsheet.

ZED
I haven't, as a matter of fact.
Just for once, I'm not going to plan.

I just shrug & say,
Come on, Marnie.
Be brave.

MARNIE
He just shrugs and says,
Be brave.

ZED
& we
rip our results open like
tearing off a plaster,
quickly, all at once.

MARNIE
And we
rip our results open like
tearing off a plaster,
quickly, all at once.

Author's Note

I wrote *Not Going to Plan* for the Marnie who is still part of me. I'm not an expert on any of the issues raised in this novel (there are some links for help below), but I was a troubled teenager, and I wish I'd had a book like this to let me know I wasn't alone.

If Marnie is a lot like the girl I once was, Zed was written as a homage to a person dear to me, someone who graciously let me bug them with questions about physics and gender identity. *Thank you.* Zed and I are very grateful for your help.

Sex is a messy business, and so is growing up. Exploring who we are, setting boundaries, trying to like and respect ourselves, deciding what we believe and how we are going to behave . . . it's a lifelong process. Zed's advice would be, don't be in a rush to define yourself or have other people define you. Give yourself space to grow.

I really wanted to explore the issue of consent. It's taken me many years to understand that my need to be wanted meant I didn't value myself highly enough – and neither did I think it was okay to change my mind about having sex when I'd already said *yes*. But it is. No one should force or trick us into doing anything we don't want to, and Marnie's experience is a reminder that we should only decide to do stuff like this when we're sober. Explicit consent has to be given by each person, at every stage of sex: it might feel unnecessary or embarrassing, but make sure it's there.

As for abortion, some girls (Rakel, for example) would never make the choice that Marnie did, and that's the right thing for them. But for others, not having a baby at this stage in their lives is the best option. In the year I researched this book, about seven thousand under-eighteen-year-old girls in the UK had abortions, and every one of them would have had their own reason for this deeply personal, difficult decision.

Although over half the teenage girls in the UK who get pregnant don't continue with the pregnancy, their stories aren't often reflected in books or films for young people, because abortion is a subject we find really, *really* hard to be open about. Because of this, young people who experience abortion may feel like they are the only ones or that they have a shameful secret to hide.

As I finish this book, I'm painfully aware that in many parts of the world women's reproductive rights are being eroded. Those of us who have the freedom to do so need to be more open about this subject, and about the choices available – because if we're not, the stigma will continue, and one day the choice may not be there.

If you find yourself in Marnie's situation, it's important to get free, non-judgemental support and advice. The sources below are a better place to start than AI.

Finally, please remember that if you decide not to go ahead with your pregnancy, you shouldn't feel ashamed. Like Marnie's mum says, learn from it.

This is your body. Your life. Your choice.

Help and Advice

Please note this information was correct at time of publication, but services do change from time to time.

For urgent help, call emergency services. If you feel your life – or the life of someone else – is in danger, you can call emergency services for free on 999 at any time of the day or night.

If you are struggling, **The Samaritans** are there to help. Call 116 123 or visit samaritans.org
Shout is a 24/7 text service for people in crisis. Text: 'SHOUT' to 85258. Visit: giveusashout.org

SEXUAL HEALTH

Brook is a sexual health and wellbeing charity which provides Relationships, Sex and Health Education, wellbeing support, and sexual healthcare for young people. Brook believes that every young person has the right to accurate information about their body and life and should be able to access confidential care and support.

You can access free, reliable advice on topics such as anatomy, contraception, pregnancy, STIs, abortion, relationships and more here: brook.org.uk

For a full list of helplines and websites addressing sexuality, abuse, wellbeing, STIs, bodies, relationships and more, visit: brook.org.uk/get-help

To find your local sexual health service, visit: brook.org.uk/find-a-service

Follow Brook on Instagram (@brook_sexpositive) and TikTok (@brookcharity) for accurate, reliable information about sex and relationships.

PREGNANCY AND ABORTION

The NHS website includes comprehensive information about pregnancy and maternity. Visit: nhs.uk/pregnancy

For information and support on **miscarriage**, visit: miscarriageassociation.org.uk

You can discuss your **pregnancy options** with your GP or a specialist service. Most abortions in the UK are provided by MSI Reproductive Choices and BPAS. In Northern Ireland, all abortions are provided by BPAS. You can visit their websites for information about abortion or ring their helplines to discuss booking an abortion, or to request counselling to help with your decision.
MSI Reproductive Choices Visit: msichoices.org.uk. Call: 0345 3008090.
BPAS Visit: bpas.org. Call: 03457 30 40 30.

Abortion Talk is a free, confidential talk line staffed by volunteers who just give you time to talk. Whether you are considering having an abortion, have had an abortion or are supporting someone in this situation, Abortion Talk volunteers are there to listen on the phone or via webchat.

Visit: abortiontalk.com Webchat: abortiontalk.com/webchat
Call: 03330 909266

Warning: some pregnancy advice centres or pregnancy crisis centres are there to persuade you not to have an abortion but won't necessarily tell you that. Unlike the reputable organisations listed above, they might not provide you with accurate information or impartial counselling.

LGBTQ + SUPPORT

Switchboard is the national LGBTQIA+ support line for anyone, anywhere in the country, at any point in their journey, for anything related to sexuality and gender identity. Whether it's sexual health, relationships or just the way you're feeling. Visit: switchboard.lgbt

LGBT Foundation – Non-judgmental support and advice on a range of topics via a dedicated helpline.
Visit: lgbt.foundation/helpline

Gendered Intelligence is a trans-led and trans-involving grassroots organisation working to increase understanding of gender diversity and improve trans people's quality of life.
Visit: genderedintelligence.co.uk

CHILDREN AND YOUNG PEOPLE (GENERAL HELP)

Childline advise and help on a wide range of issues for anyone aged 19 or under: call free on 0800 1111 or chat 1-2-1 via Childline's website at childline.org.uk

Barnados – A wide range of support for children and their families (including mental health and LGBTQ+ services, and help if you're struggling to afford the essentials).
Visit: barnardos.org.uk

The Mix offers free, confidential digital help and support for anyone aged 13 to 25. Text 'THEMIX' to 85258 for text-based support. Visit: themix.org.uk

CAREERS OPTIONS

The King's Trust (formerly The Prince's Trust) offers courses, resources and other support to help people aged 11 to 30 to develop essential life skills, get ready for work and access job opportunities. Visit: kingstrust.org.uk. Webchat: kingstrust.org.uk/how-we-can-help/get-in-touch
Call: 0800 842 842.

Acknowledgements

I've wanted to write this book for a long time. I'm so grateful to my agent Eve White and my editor Emma Matthewson for recognising that *Not Going to Plan* is an important story which needs to be read by young people.

Thanks to the brilliant Talya Baker – who understands formatting, voice, and the importance of detail like no one else – and to every member of the Hot Key Books team who has endured the madness of this text and my illustrative whims. A deep bow also to the design, PR, marketing and sales people who are working so hard to get this book into the world and a salute to the librarians and teachers for (I hope) having the courage to introduce it to their young people.

I couldn't have written this without research, and I'm indebted to the following for giving up their time: the Brook charity, who offer advice and education on sexual health and wellbeing; my niece who devotes her working life to helping young women in Trump's America access abortion care; Amy and Viv, who work on the frontline in NHS clinics; artists Jane Spencer and Sam Halpenny, who generously taught me about screen printing; and finally my nerdy family, who filled me in on the physics.

Writing a book about abortion is a bit scary, so big thanks to Kelly McCaughrain, who gave me some much-needed emotional bolstering. Feedback and suggestions from my beta-reading crit-givers really shaped *Not Going to Plan*, and I'm enormously grateful to writers Cathy Faulkner, A. Connors, Margaret McDonald, Steve Voake (in whose workshop I got the idea for the Wall of Words) and the MAWFYers. Also to my teen readers: Emma, Stan and '*it's an everything cocktail!*' Mia.

I'm lucky enough to have some very special girlfriends – who supported me through my own unplanned pregnancy many, many years ago – and an amazing husband, who puts up with all my writing nonsense and cooks like a dream.

Thank you all.

Discussion points for book clubs and reading groups, RSHE, PSHE, and English classrooms

1. One of the themes of *Not Going to Plan* is making mistakes. How do Marnie and Zed's approaches to making mistakes differ, and do they change over the course of the book?

2. Marnie and Harry are over the legal age of consent in this country (sixteen years old). Why do you think we have an age of consent? How does it help young people, and is it set at the right age?

3. On page 305, Marnie says, 'We're damned if we do/damned if we don't.' Do you agree with Marnie and Rakel that there is a stigma attached to both girls who want to have sex *and* to girls who don't?

4. On pages 288 and 289, Zed lists some of the differing opinions about when life begins. Why do you think there is such a wide range of opinions about abortion? How well do you think those views are represented in *Not Going to Plan*?

5. To what degree do you think Marnie and Harry were each responsible for Marnie's unplanned pregnancy? Is there anyone else you think also bears responsibility?

6. Had you heard of 'stealthing' before reading the book? Why do you think the law was changed so that lying about using a condom is classed as rape?

7. What do you think of Marnie's decision not to tell Harry about her pregnancy?

8. Why do you think the author created such different single-parent backgrounds for Marnie and Zed? What effect do you think this might have on their outlooks?

9. Do you have sympathy for the character of Jessica Bates? Why do you feel that way?

10. On page 312, Luca expresses regret that he didn't do more to protect others against the homophobia in his school. Do you think we all have a responsibility towards anybody who is bullied or excluded because of who they are; for example, for their looks, their sexuality, their gender, etc.?

11. Do you think Marnie's reasons for not wanting to tell her mother about her pregnancy and subsequent abortion were justifiable? How would you have felt about this if you were Marnie's mother?

12. Zed resists the idea of being labelled as anything. Why do you think we like to give others – and even ourselves – identity labels?

13. The book is written in narrative verse. How do you think reading a book in verse is different to reading a story told in conventional prose? What do the illustrations and shape poems add to your appreciation of the text? Do you think the two interweaving voices would have been as effective in prose?

14. What was the result of Marnie relying solely on AI sources of information about her suspected pregnancy? What else could she have done?

15. Do you think the young people in *Not Going to Plan* could have avoided some of their negative experiences if they had had better Relationships, Sex and Health Education? What has been good about the RSHE you have had in your school and what could be better?

16. What should parents'/carers' roles be in supporting, talking to or educating their children about things like relationships, contraception, abortion, sexuality, etc.?

17. If you had a friend who needed advice but didn't want to talk to a parent or teacher about their situation, where would you suggest they get help?

18. Did you learn anything from reading *Not Going to Plan*?

There are more resources aimed at schools for both
Not Going to Plan and *Crossing the Line*
at tiafisher.com

About the Author

Tia Fisher writes books for the rebel inside her. She spent her youth desperate to escape the boredom of a tiny village in Norfolk, writing poems of love and rebellion and reading indiscriminately through the shelves of the local library. After being expelled from boarding school and dropping out of university, Tia had a bewildering variety of jobs – from TV presenter to ESOL teacher to artists' model – before finding her happy place working in libraries and writing stories. In her fifties she went back to university, and is now the proud owner of a master's degree in writing for young people. She recently moved back to Norwich and now she loves it.

Tia's debut teen verse novel, *Crossing the Line*, was the winner of the 2024 Carnegie Shadowers' Choice Medal and the UKLA 11-14+ prize, and is in the 2024 Reading for Empathy collection. In 2026 Piccadilly Press will publish Tia's debut middle-grade story, *Operation Doodlebug*, which is set in World War Two.

Tia's website (with resources to support *Not Going to Plan* and *Crossing the Line*) is at tiafisher.com. Tia's socials can be found at linktr.ee/tiafisherwrites.

CROSSING THE LINE

This is the story of Erik...
he's very good at making
bad decisions

TIA FISHER

Read on for an extract ...

Seems like bad decisions

stack like dominoes.
When one topples, they all go.
    Clackety-
        clackety-
            clackety-
                clackety-
                    clackety-
                        clackety-
                            clackety-
                              clackety-
                                CLACK,
                                    all the way down.

Looking back,
maybe this was
    the first domino to topple?

The mis_{step}
    that kicked off
    the run.

I think this must be a record!

The head teacher's lips
    crinkle tight
like the drawstring of a shoe bag.
He narrows his eyes.

Shouts drift up
    from the field
        & bounce off the window.

                              It's break time already.
                        I've spent the whole first period
                                   sitting like an idiot
                            outside Mr Nelson's office.

It's the first time
   ANYONE has EVER
been sent to see me
   for fighting
     on their very first day!
he says.

                                        I bet it isn't.

Outside, a group of
   boys weave a tight knot
     in the far corner of the field.
Smoke curls a wispy signal.

Actually –
the head teacher
   checks his watch
     for effect –
in their very first hour.

                         I run my tongue around my
                                   mashed-up mouth
                        but Mr Nelson doesn't invite me
                                        to open it
                                   in self-defence.

When the head teacher finally

lets me go,
I spend ages looking for
    the geography room
where I'm supposed to have
    period three.

All the corridors
    look the same,
ghost-town empty of
    their teenage traffic.

When I finally
    locate Room G3,
I tap on the door
    as quietly as I can.

A tall, bearded teacher
    is standing by the board.
He nods curtly at me
    to enter.

He makes me sit alone
    on a table at the front
while he talks about
    archipelagos.

I'm marooned
    on this island
    in a sea full of stares.

I can feel my ears burning,
    red as my hair.

Having red hair is *not* OK!

We should've
    dyed it,
        shaved it,
            waxed or wigged it –
made up some excuse,
said I was having chemo or something.

No one should've
    allowed me to believe
    there was nothing
    wrong with me.

Why didn't someone tell me
    having red hair is not okay?

My best friend looks

embarrassed
    as we file into lunch.

Sorry, he says,
picking up a small plastic tray
    spattered with
    someone else's gravy.
Sorry I didn't help back there.

                    S'okay, I say, fishing out my fob
                    & wondering what I'm supposed
                                    to do with it.
                            *You're not exactly
                                a fighter* . . .

How about, says Ravi,
pointing to the veggie option
& smiling at the dinner lady,
next time
    you keep your big gob shut
        instead?

Erik, there was actual *blood!*

I should have known
    Mum'd get a call:
as soon as I walk in
    she's on at me –

She's so shocked
she doesn't even ask
    about my day.

                But, Mum . . .
                I start –
        but she won't let me finish.

              I want to say
            I can still taste my fear,
      the push of his arm pressed
                across my neck,
my heartbeat thud-thudding in my ears.

              Pinned to the wall
        by painful rabbit punches,
              I couldn't breathe,
              I couldn't *breathe* –

              Of course I bit him.
              It was self-defence.